# THE MOST EXCITING STORY OF THE DAY.

Nos. 1 & 2]
[One Penny.]

# BLACK WOLF;

OR,

## THE BOY HIGHWAYMAN.

[THE RESCUE OF ALICE WAYNCLIFFE.]

BEAUTIFULLY ILLUSTRATED.

No. 2 GRATIS WITH No. 1.     ONE PENNY WEEKLY.

OFFICE: 125, FLEET STREET, LONDON.

# BLACK WOLF;

OR,

## THE BOY HIGHWAYMAN.

THE RESCUE OF ALICE WAYNCLIFFE.

## CHAPTER I.

### AN ADVENTURE ON THE ROAD.

IT was a clear starry night!

A night for peaceful thoughts and lonely wanderings beneath the twinkling lights of heaven—a night when the moon glimmered down and lit with its clear subdued glow the tall swaying trees, and brought out in strong relief the dark shadow of a young horseman, who stood alone on the silent highway.

No. 1.

A boy—a bold handsome fellow of about sixteen years of age, who sat like a statue upon a powerful steed whose glossy hide was as black as the raven's wing.

A noble majestic-looking creature it was, faultless of limb, and with wide deep flanks and chest, a long silken mane and finely-curved neck, a small head, short ears, and proud fiery eye; swift of pace as the wild antelope, yet quiet and docile as a lamb.

Docile! yet only so to its master.

Not another foot dared to touch the stirrup save that of his present rider, and the gallant steed would brook no stranger on his back.

Selim—such was the name bestowed by the youth upon his favourite—knew the sound of his master's voice or footstep as well as ever maiden knew the voice or footstep of her lover, and no woman ever loved a man more faithfully than did the noble Selim love his master.

By the horse's feet, with his huge head resting on his paws, there lay a huge mastiff, whose skin, like his companion's, was as black as night, and, like the horse, he was a handsome fellow in his way.

He had a massive head, with a strong deep jaw: a quiet watchful eye, and for strength and swiftness he was incomparable.

That dog loved his master with a devotion almost human, and was ever on the alert to warn him of coming danger, or defend him when it came.

That princely-looking boy stood in need of two such friends, for the life he led was a wild life of peril.

You could see it in the glitter of his dark flashing eye, and the calm fearless daring of his handsome face—you could see that danger was to him a joyous sense of wild excitement, as he sat there so statue-like and still, looking back and listening intently, while one hand rested on the jewelled hilt of his sword.

Selim stood as though carved in marble, and, with his ears bent back as though he, too, was listening; and the black mastiff seemed so watchful and intent that it could be seen that he listened like the others.

It came again!

The distant sound of two or more equestrians riding rapidly down the road.

Coming swiftly towards the youth awaiting their approach. About half a mile a-head of where he stood, the road sloped upwards into a hill of considerable height, and over this the first rider came to view, followed on the instant by two others.

The foremost of the three was a lady; the other two were men—gentlemen, by their rich attire and general appearance.

At least so far as could be seen, for the faces of both were masked.

One glance as they came on told the boy the purpose of their ride, and his dark eye flashed as his sword left its sheath.

"Two ruffians in pursuit of a lady: a helpless girl, perchance!" he muttered, "Wolf, old fellow! we are wanted to the rescue."

A touch upon the rein and Selim turned to face the lady and the others as they came.

Black Wolf sat back upon his haunches, and bared his white fangs as he heared his master speak.

The lady had now come so near that the boy could see her white lovely face pale with fear at the thought of being overtaken by her dastardly pursuers.

But as her gaze fell upon the handsome features and rich costly dress of the young horseman, a look of hope brought a glow to her checks, and she exclaimed

"Save me! oh, save me!"

"From whom, sweet lady?"

"From those men—I do not know them; but I know that their intent is evil—you will not let them take me now?"

"Not while I live."

He had not time to say more.

The foremost of the maiden's two pursuers was within fifty yards of his intended prey.

He did not for an instant think that the slight graceful youth to whom the lady had just spoken would dare to interrupt him. He did not think so until he found himself suddenly compelled to rein in.

His eyes gleamed fiercely through the holes of his mask, and a muttered oath broke from his lips.

"Stand aside," he shouted.

"Not yet," was the cool reply.

"Curses," exclaimed the other, savagely, "let me pass, or I will cut you down!"

The boy laughed lightly as he pulled Selim across the road in such a manner as to completely bar the way.

He held his sword with the point resting lightly on his saddle, and sat regarding the two strangers with a look of quiet daring, which evinced a strong and calm determination to keep them back.

The maiden trembled in every limb, with fear for the life of her young defender.

They formed a strange picture as they stood thus together.

The two masked horsemen, standing side by side, and staring savagely at the boy, who kept them from the object of their pursuit, and he, sword in hand, sitting motionless on his sable steed, underneath which Black Wolf crouched down, ready to leap at the throat of the first who dared to move a step towards his master.

Like two savage tigers brought suddenly to bay by a daring hunter, stood the maiden's masked pursuers, eager for their prey, yet not daring to advance, because of that gallant boy's gleaming sword, and the strong white fangs of the noble hound who crouched beneath his horse.

"Well, gentlemen," said the boy at length, "may I ask what you want with this lady?"

"She is my daughter," replied the foremost of the two, speaking in a voice which was evidently assumed for the occasion, "why she has left her home I do not know, nor have you a right to question."

"Cut him down!" exclaimed the other, "how dare he stand thus between a father and his child!"

"It is false!" said the maiden; "he is not my father."

"It scarcely needs your word to tell me that," said the youth; the assertion of the first who spoke seemed so very like a lie that I should not care to trust you to his parental care. Now, gentlemen, stand back; I have no time to waste with you; and having seen the lady safe from your clutches I must attend to my own interesting occupation; stand back!"

But neither of the masked riders moved an inch.

There was a dark murderous gleam in the eye of the elder as the dauntless youth dashed forward.

"Shoot him down!" he cried to his companion, as with his own sword he crossed that of his young antagonist; "damnation, the girl will escape!"

Such, indeed, seemed a very probable occurrence.

In obedience to his companion's kind instruction, the second gentlemanly ruffian had drawn a pistol from his belt, and took deliberate aim at the boy's white forehead.

But before he could pull the trigger, Black Wolf gave a deep fierce growl, and, leaping right at his throat, bore him to the ground. The ball went harmlessly upward, and the baffled ruffian lay stunned by the heavy fall, while the huge mastiff sat quietly on his chest, and growled to himself with much satisfaction.

He seemed to know that his master was quite safe while he had to fight with only one antagonist; but he watched the progress of the conflict with an expression on his face of more than dog-like sagacity, and kept his teeth bound ready to pin his captive, if, on his return to consciousness, he should make any attempt to rise.

Meanwhile, the contest between the other two continued with such desperation as to threaten to have a fatal termination.

The mask was a powerful man, and could use his weapon well; but the boy's supple wrist was like iron in its strength, and he held his own with a skill and coolness which, in one so young, was literally marvellous.

But it was not the first time that he had fought hand to hand, for on many occasions before this, he had defended his life against fearful odds.

He had gained his masterly knowledge of the science of the sword by stern practice alone.

So cool he was, yet so quick in parrying the rapid heavy strokes of his exasperated foe, that you could see his skill was inherent, like his fearlessness, and he seemed to like the peril and excitement of the fight.

Which the other did not.

He had tried every trick of fence known to the most expert, and found himself met at every point.

"Curses!" he muttered between his teeth; "if it were not for the infernal hound I should not have to fight this devil by myself."

"You are getting tired," said the boy, as he still kept the other actively at work. "well, then, let us end our contest."

So saying he drew a pistol from beneath his coat.

It was a splendid weapon, with a long slender barrel, which glistened like burnished steel.

The butt was richly set with massive silver.

It looked very handsome, with its chased costly sittings and glistening tube, but it was dangerous oftimes, as its owner could have told.

There was many others, too, who could have seconded his tale.

There was just the shadow of a smile on the boy's handsome face as he drew the weapon forth—a smile of mocking sarcasm, called into life by the look of fear in the quailing eye of his opponent. Unknown to any sense of fear himself he could only smile thus at any man who could let such a feeling dwell within his heart.

There was a look of mischief in his dark eye, and all the light and beauty of his face seemed to die out, and have such a stern strange pitiless expression that the strong man whom he fought shuddered as he saw it.

He thought that his time had come.

In truth it would have been so with him, for the deadly tube was levelled at his heart, and the next moment would have seen him stricken stark and bleeding from his horse but for the sweet plaintive voice of the maiden whom he had so savagely pursued.

"Do not kill him," she said, pained she knew not why by the cold deadly look which gleamed out from every lineament of her young preserver's face, "do not, for my sake; do not stain your hand with blood."

"Not kill him!" said the boy, as he turned aside a desperate thrust made by the other, "not kill him, lady, why it would be mercy perhaps compared with that which he would have done to you."

But her gentle intercession saved the other's life, for the young horseman turned aside his deadly aim.

"For your sweet sake," he said, "I will not kill him."

Even while he found time to speak thus, he was never for an instant off his guard.

His gleaming weapon flashed and circled with such rapidity that his antagonist grew at last bewildered.

The boy could have slain him more than once, but faithful to the word he had given he was content to let him live.

One thing, however, he wished to do before they parted.

He felt a strong wish to know the identity of the man with whom he battled, and so that he might do so should they meet at any time; the boy resolved to set a mark upon him.

By an imperceptible touch he made Selim leap forward suddenly, and with a swift powerful turn of the wrist he sent the other's sword whirling from his hand, and his own weapon gleamed again like a flash of lightning as it flashed upward, and cut the masked man just above the temple. Cutting through the mask which covered his face it made a gash, which the boy well knew would leave an indelible scar—a mark like the brand of Cain upon the brow of his unknown antagonist.

The wounded man reeled in the saddle, but recovering himself by a mighty effort he rode away to some little distance, and exclaimed fiercely, "Curse you for this! we shall meet again, and then look to it, for I will have your heart's blood."

"Will you?" laughed the daring boy as he sheathed his sword, "Well, when we meet again see that you keep your promise. I shall know you, let it be when and where it may; and we shall meet again, and that too when you least expect it."

Then he turned to the trembling girl.

"Lady," he said in a strangely soft musical voice, "you are safe now, and I shall be most happy if you will suffer me to escort you to your home."

"Many thanks," replied the maiden, blushing beneath his ardent gaze, "in truth I know not how to thank you for your gallant kindness, and my uncle I am sure will be proud to welcome one who has dared so much to save his niece."

The boy bowed gracefully in reply, and then turned to see how it fared with the captive of whom Black Wolf was taking such especial care. He had recovered now, and occasionally gave a dismal groan, as every time he raised his head the dog gave him a heavy pat on the jaw with his huge paw and knocked it down again, giving a growl each time as though he rather liked the situation.

This gratifying process had been repeated until the captive's head had made quite a dent in the ground; and as he gave a groan at every pat, and got a pat for every groan, there was every prospect of the dent soon being made of sufficient depth to hold his head, had not the youth took compassion on the miserably piteous spectacle he presented, and called Wolf away.

Being thus relieved of his charge the mastiff wagged his tail and looked sagaciously at his master, then took an affectionate leave of his prisoner, by first taking the greater part of his scarf and a little of his neck in his teeth, and giving him a very solemn and impressive shaking; then administering a farewell pat which sent his captive's head deep into the dent, and caused it (the head not the dent) to ache for many days, and having done this the mastiff slowly rose from the chest of the prostrate man and took his place by the side of Selim, who had been looking on as though he very much approved of the whole affair, particularly the part in which his comrade was concerned.

We say comrade—for Black Wolf and Selim were on the best of terms—they shared the same stable when at home, drank from the same trough, and doubtless would have eaten of the same food, only Black Wolf being a very serious dog did not care for chaff—to which Selim was particularly partial.

They were staunch and faithful friends nevertheless, and next to their affection for their master came their affection for each other.

To return, however to our hero.

As the second of his fair companion's pursuers mounted his horse, the youth exclaimed, "You will find your friend down the road, and so good night, but when next you attack a lady be careful that you do not come in contact with Black Wolf, or his master."

With a muttered oath the other rode away, followed by the boy's merry laugh, and a growl from the mastiff, who looked longingly after his late prisoner.

"May I ask to whom I have been so fortunate as to render this slight service," asked our hero.

"My name is Alice Wayncliffe," was the reply, "my uncle is Lord Wayncliffe, of Wayncliffe Grange."

"Wayncliffe," repeated her companion meditatively, "surely I have heard that name before."

"My uncle is the celebrated judge of whom you have perhaps heard mention," said Alice, "Judge Wayncliffe he is generally called, and as such you have doubtless heard the name."

"Most probable," rejoined the boy, wincing at the answers, and here he turned the conversation.

Alice said but little, but not a word was lost that her companion uttered, for never before had she listened unto one whose converse possessed such a charm, or whose voice was so soft and winning.

She was just lost in thought as to who and what this handsome young stranger could be, when they drew rein at the Grange.

Lord Wayncliffe, who had been alarmed by the protracted absence of his neice, despatched messengers in all directions to search for her, welcomed her gladly back, and gazed with a strange wondering look at her companion, a shadow of deep sadness gathered on his brow, as though the sight of that boy's handsome face touched him to the heart with the memory of some bygone sorrow.

He listened with a look of pleased interest to the glowing tale told by Alice of her companion's gallant skill and daring, and when she had concluded her recital, he took our hero's hand.

"You are welcome, gladly welcome," he said, and the words came from his heart, "and should the time ever come that you need a friend, let that friend be Godfrey Wayncliffe."

The boy gazed earnestly into his face.

"If ever such a time should come," he said, "I shall not forget those words."

"I trust you will not," said Lord Wayncliffe, and as Selim and the other horse were led away by the groom, he took his niece and our hero into the Grange, "and now let me know who it is I have to thank for the safety of my child."

"My name is Wilford Leander," replied our hero. "I am brother to Captain Rolfe Leander, late of the Mexican Rangers."

Black Wolf, who had followed them in, looked up as he heard his master speak the name of Captain Rolfe, then resting his head on his huge paws he gazed wistfully into Wilford's face.

The boy understood that look and would have taken his departure, but he had to yield at last to the urgent request that he should stay, which was given by Lord Wayncliffe and the lovely Alice.

Then he bent down and caressed his faithful dog with much affection as he said—

"Not to night, old fellow, not to night, there is plenty of time for that."

---

## CHAPTER II.

### LORD WAYNCLIFFE OF WAYNCLIFFE.

"You will not leave us yet, I hope?" said Lord Wayncliffe, as on the evening after that on which he had rescued Alice from the masked horsemen the young stranger said that he must depart for a time, much to the disappointment both of the peer and the fair Alice, who in her gratitude to her youthful champion, did not wish to see him go so soon; and though the brave boy felt flattered by her solicitude and her uncle's kindness, he urged his temporary absence as a matter of necessity, and Lord Wayncliffe was too well bred to press the subject.

"I must ride to London," said Wilford, "but believe me, I am too sensible of the pleasure offered by your kindness to stay away longer than I have occasion: I will return to-morrow night."

"In safety, I hope," said Lord Wayncliffe, "you are going a dangerous road, if report speaks true, for it has been said that the Black Wolf has been seen lately on the very road you are about to take?"

"They mean my dog, perhaps," said the boy, with a peculiar smile, "as to that tale of that half-human monster, I can scarcely give it credence."

"It is true beyond a doubt, I believe," said the peer, "in fact more than one gentleman of my acquaintance has been stopped by him, and plundered on the highway."

"Indeed! how have they described him," asked Wilford, "there are so many tales afloat concerning his appearance that it is difficult to ascertain the truth."

"Those who have told me of their adventures with

him have given as near as possible the same account and it is a strange one too."

"Dreadful!" said Alice, with a shudder.

"Yet," said the boy, with a second strange smile. "I have heard that the brute, or whatever he may be, is singularly gallant in all occasions wherein a lady is concerned."

"I should die with fright at the very thought of being touched by him," said Alice, while her uncle smiled, and Wilford said—

"I trust that may never be your fate, though if it were, your beauty would tame him into gentleness; but, my lord, you have not yet told us what he is like."

"Like a wolf, so they say," replied Wayncliffe, "a strange half-demoniac creature whom nature has created, as it were, to strike fear and wonder into the hearts of all who saw it; its limbs and feet are perfect, but the hands are like the paws of the animal he is said to resemble, while its head, without having the projecting muzzle, is wolfish in every lineament, with hairy human ears, strong white tusks and teeth, and red glittering eyes that glare like the orbs of a fiend —a thing it is altogether horrible to imagine, and still more horrible to see."

"So I should think by that," said Wilford, who had listened with much curiosity to the description, "I should much like to meet him, does he go on foot?"

"No, he is magnificently mounted; he rides a beautiful Arabian, a black splendid creature, with a white star on his forehead and another on his breast; such another horse as yours, I should think, in point of built and breed, without the stars, of course."

"It is fortunate my Selim has no stars," said Wilford, with a laugh, "or the resemblance might lead me into difficulties."

Lord Wayncliffe smiled, and Alice chimed in with her low musical laugh at the idea of the handsome youth before them being taken for such a hideous monster as the Black Wolf.

"But it is somewhat of a coincidence," said the peer, "that besides the black Arabian he should have a dog which, if description is correct, must be the very fac simile of this young noble mastiff."

"A coincidence more strange still that my dog should bear the same appellation as that borne by this semi-human highwayman," said Wilford, with another laugh, "really, if the resemblance comes much nearer, I shall have to ride about with my credentials in my pocket. That reminds me, my lord, that as yet you know little of him you have honoured by your confidence and friendship. I have told you my name, and that of my only relative, my brother, for the next I must refer you to the king."

"The king!" exclaimed Lord Wayncliffe in surprise, while Alice felt her heart fluttering at the thought that Wilford might be a prince in disguise.

"His Majesty King George the First," replied the youth gravely, "I wear this ring given by him to me in token of a service I once rendered him."

He took from his finger a golden circlet, set with one costly diamond, and inside the slender hoop the words "George, Rex," where engraved in minute letters, while a miniature copy of the royal crest was delicately carved on the inside of the part wherein the jewel rested.

"It does not need such proof as this to tell you that you are a gentleman," said his lordship, who nevertheless felt pleased that the youth could give such evidence of his birth and position; and even were you not, your gallant conduct gives you a strong claim upon my gratitude. I can only add that Wayncliffe Grange is open to you always, and that, come when or how you may, you shall be welcome."

"You are very kind, Lord Wayncliffe," said Wilford, and a thrill ran through his frame as the other took his hand; "such a promise is very grateful unto me, being as I am, almost alone in the world. Forgive me, my lord, if I presume too much when I say that, had it pleased fate to let me know a father's love, I should wish that father were Lord Wayncliffe."

He spoke earnestly, for his heart felt what his tongue uttered; but he paused with surprise when, feeling the peer's hand tighten on his own, he looked up and saw that his eyes were dim with tears.

Alice came to her uncle's side, and looked wonderingly at the pair, while Black Wolf raised his head, and looked on with an expression of sympathy almost human.

"Your words have struck upon a chord which until now has for many years remained untouched," Lord Wayncliffe said, after they had stood some time in silence, "and while it yet thrills I will tell you a story which I have never told before, and which is only known to those who knew it when first the sad event occurred. It is fourteen years ago," he continued, "since the blow fell which left me a childless man. I had been in London for several days engaged on a trial, leaving the Grange meanwhile in charge of my wife. My brother and a friend of his, Lord Henry Rivers, were staying with me at the time, and I left them altogether as many times, and had left them before; but treachery and wrong is ever the inheritance of trust: and on the last day of the trial, just when I was about to return, I received a letter from my brother, telling me that my wife had fled in company with Lord Rivers, and with them they had taken my child, a little boy, then two years old. Doubting all, save my wife's fidelity, I returned home at once, where I saw my brother in a state bordering on distraction, for the affectionate fellow knew with what fearful weight such tidings would fall upon my heart. They had gone, he said, in the night, and he had searched in vain for a clue by which he might trace them. We searched, but in vain; they were gone: yet even then I did not doubt my wife. I do not doubt her now, and would stake my soul that she was true. I may never gaze again upon her face, and, perhaps, my child may never be restored to me; but I will never cast a slur on her name, for I am certain that there is some awful mystery connected with their disappearance, which God, in his own good time, will bring to light. I have told this to you, Wilford, because your face reminds me of the face of her who has so long been lost; and when I first saw you I thought that, if my boy were living, he would be like yourself, for you are all I could have wished to see him."

A change came over Wilford's face as he heard the last words, and for a moment he remained silent.

Silent with a sad feeling of regret that he could not in truth take those words unto himself.

Then he said—

"I would to heaven that I were now worthy of your trust; and I can well appreciate that noble thought that would not let you doubt your wife. It was a just one, as I feel assured time will prove, and, in return for your confidence, I swear that to the utmost I will strive to elucidate the mystery. Farewell, my lord; farewell, sweet lady; to-morrow night I shall return. And now for a ride to London, and a meeting, I hope, with the Black Wolf."

A groom stood at the door, holding Selim's rein, and, waving his hand to Alice and her uncle, who stood by the window, Wilford mounted the Arabian, and rode away, closely followed by the mastiff.

"Well, Alice," said Lord Wayncliffe, as the young rider was lost to view, "what think you of your champion?"

A vivid blush mounted to the maiden's lily cheeks, and, drawing her to his breast, her uncle said—

"You must not lose your heart yet, my birdie: remember it is scarcely twenty-four hours since you first beheld him."

Alice did not speak; had she done so, she might have told him that his warning had come too late.

It does not take a lady long to fall in love, especially under such circumstances as those under which Alice met our hero.

"It was strange that you should have been so attacked," said Lord Wayncliffe, after a pause; "did you not know either of them from the voice?"

"They were disguised in every way," replied Alice, "and I think they were strangers—highwaymen, perhaps."

"Perhaps so; they sprang, you say, from behind a hedge, and tried to seize your horse's bridle?"

"They did; but he started, and they missed. In my terror I knew not where to go. I ably kept my seat, and rode as fast as I could."

"The best course, as it chanced," said the peer. "Thanks to our gallant young friend; he at least will recognise one of the miscreants."

"How?" asked Alice.

"By the mark upon his brow," replied Lord Wayncliffe.

---

## CHAPTER III.

### BLACK WOLF.

ALTHOUGH it was late before Wilford started from Wayncliffe Grange he did not seem at all terrified by the supposition that he might meet with the terrible creature known as the Black Wolf.

It must have been a strange fancy that which prompted him to give his faithful dog the same name as that borne by the weird monster who was often the terror of the road, but Wilford Leander was a strange fellow, and did strange things more strange than that.

The distance between the Grange and London was not very great, for in the time of our story Lord Wayncliffe's house stood near Richmond Park.

In fact, had the boy wished to do so, he could have reached London in one hour, but he did not seem at all in haste.

Having got out of sight of the house he had just left, he let Selim drop into a walk, and he himself fell into a reverie.

A sad one for the time it seemed, if his thoughts might be judged by the expression of his handsome face.

"I am sixteen to-day," he muttered as he rode, "and a strange way of life is mine, it is just one year since I took to the road, and in that time I have made myself a name which has echoed through the land. A wild career, and have known and have gloried in it until now—and never until I met Lord Wayncliffe and that lovely girl have I thought upon it with regret. Why should I do so now? I never wronged a fellow creature in my life; yet for the sake of Alice I could wish that I had not been doomed to such a destiny; she loves me—heaven help her—and even were she to know me as I am, I feel assured that she would link her fate with my own desperate fortunes; but I love her, at least too well for that, and in that love I would not cloud the light of her young life by taking her from her uncle's house to make her—what?—a felon's bride, a felon's bride," he repeated bitterly, "yet what I do is justified by the world's law, at the sword's point I make the rich man yield his gold—for the poor my hand is ever at my purse."

His thoughts changed here, and for some time he rode on in silence, then again he broke into his muttered soliloquy, and continued—

"A strange story was that Lord Wayncliffe told me, wife, child, and friend, all lost—there is a mystery in that which I may help to fathom. I would give much to fathom that in which my own life is clouded. I never knew my parents, and Captain Rolfe, kind and devoted as to me he is, is not my brother, nor is he that which he would wish to seem, he has a native pride of soul which tells that he is a gentleman by birth in spite of what fate has made him now; by the way, I forget that I have to meet him at the Den; but first I must look out for a little business on my own account."

He gently touched the neck of the Arabian, who went forward with a bound, and kept rapidly onward until he reached the door of a road-side Inn where Selim stopped as if by instinct.

Wilford dismounted, and patting the horse's glossy neck, strode into the Inn.

Wolf took his companion's rein in his mouth and sat down to wait for his master

The Inn at which they were was called "The Shepherd and His Dog." This much any intellectual traveller might have gathered from a lengthened study of the signboard, wherein was painted the figure of an individual who looked like a distant relation to the man in the moon, that is to say, according to the usual artistic rendering of that popular public-house character who is generally seen with a bundle of sticks under his arm, together with a toma-hawk-like chopper, with which he is supposed to have cut the aforesaid sticks, after which it may be pre-sumed he cut his own, and the portrait is made com-plete by a short pipe being inserted in one corner of the wanderer's mouth, and a fugitive dog, who keeps his nose close to the ground as though keenly on the smell for some meat which we may suppose is not retailed in small quantities in any district of that particularly thin part of the moon on which man and dog are generally placed.

In this case the man had his hands stuck in his pockets in that desperate sort of way which made him look as though he had lost himself, and did not care whether he was found again or not.

Change the scene from the thin end of the moon to something like what Shakspearse in Macbeth pro-foundly calls a blasted heath, and there you have the portraiture exact; the eternal man in the same miserable attitude—with pipe, chopper, and sticks,—and at his heels the wretched tike, who cannot find the remnant of a single skewer by which to trace any of that sliced article usually devoted to the masti-catory use of the canine population.

Underneath the artist had painted these words, in a style something between old English and strong Roman capitals—

"The Shepherd and his Dog,"

Which, if you read first, would tell you what the figures were intended for.

And while Black Wolf was regarding with a look of profound contempt the painted libel on his species, Wilford Leander was talking to mine host, who was a living libel to *his* species.

His name was John Long; and like most names it was entirely misappropriate, for he was very short, very fat, and very ugly.

Ugly is the word.

His face was at first sight totally without expres-sion; his eyes small and piggish in their character, and his nose was decidly snout-like.

Then he wore his hair cropped close to his head, either because he was afraid of its fiery colour, or else because he may have thought that large ears were an attribute of beauty; in which case his would have been very handsome.

They nearly covered each side of his head, and stopped the progress of the slit between his nose and chin.

The formidable slit did duty for his mouth.

Strange to say Long Jack, as he was called in derision by his customers, had got a wife.

By what means he contrived to win her is a mystery, which we cannot hope to elucidate.

And he had also got a daughter.

The mystery of that was not so deep; but the girl was pretty: a quiet modest girl she was, with a soft pliant form, not deficient in grace, a pair of blue innocent eyes, and a rosy little mouth which suggested kissing at the first glimpse.

Wilford was well known apparently, and he seemed to be a welcome guest to all, particularly so to the girl of whom we have just spoken, for her fair cheek grew crimson as he entered, and her little heart beat at an extraordinary rate.

"Hollo, Captain!" said the landlord, "glad to see you; wondered where you'd got to."

"Did you," said Wilford, as he kicked open the little door which led to the parlour; "well, what news have you now I am here."

While he spoke he had taken a seat, and drawn the girl to his knee; having done which, he drew her face to his and took a long kiss from her dewy lips.

"I say, Captain," said the landlord seriously, "you ain't doing right by that gal."

"Mr. Long," said Wilford gravely, "if you grow impertinent I shall kick you out of the room; what do you mean?"

"Just what I say; when you are here you go on like that with her; then you goes away and we don't see you for weeks, sometimes months, and there she sets in the corner fretting her heart out about you; t'aint right you know."

"Not that she should fret her heart out certainly," replied Wilford, with his usual nonchalance; "why, Bessie, this is not true, is it?"

The poor girl blushed, and her eyes filled with tears.

"In course it is," said her father, "which it isn't right of you to make her; you won't marry her your-self, and since you've got to taking notice of her, she won't have anybody else."

"Why should she?" said the youth, pressing the girl more closely to him, "I have never wronged her, nor ever will; I come to see her as often as I can, and that is all you wish, is it not, Bessie?"

A look of love and confidence answered him, and turning to her father he continued—

"So let us be happy while we may, my friend. How is trade with you, and what travellers have you had this way?"

"Trade!" growled the landlord, "why its going to the devil; people don't dare come out after dark."

"Why not?"

"Why the Black Wolf's been seen down this way."

"When?"

"Most every night for a week; people don't mind such gentlemen as you, who does it all polite, but when it comes to something as ain't neither man nor beast, and can't be shot when a pistol's put within a yard of him, why it's time for people to stay at home and go to bed."

Wilford laughed as he threw a handful of gold to the discontented host.

"That will make up for what you have lost through the Black Wolf's visit," he said, "now bring a bottle of your best, and help me to drink it, I shall get it good by that, for you won't poison yourself."

"I always do bring my best out for you," said boniface, as, with twinkling eyes, he pocketed the money. "I always act square with them as acts square by me."

"All right, old boy! toddle down into the cellar for a bottle or two; don't break your neck, you can afford to wait until that is done for you."

The landlord disappeared down a trap door, on his way to the cellar, and left Wilford alone with his daughter.

"Your father seems suspicious," said the boy, "you must be more careful, Bessie, as he may guess too near at the cause of your sadness when I am absent."

"I cannot help it," replied the girl tearfully, "ah, Wilford! if I thought you would deceive me I should die."

An expression of regret passed over the boy's handsome face, and, looking tenderly into his com-panion's face, he said—

"I shall not deceive you, but you must not always be in tears when you do not see me."

"But sometimes I think that you can never care

for me," said Bessie, sorrowfully. "and I fear that you may meet with a rich lady, who will make you forget all about poor Bessie!"

"What if I were to?"

He asked the question with an air half jesting, half earnest, and the girl trembled as she replied—

"It is all I can expect: but I don't care if you will always care for me a little—come and see me sometimes—I could bear it then—so that you don't forget me altogether."

A sad young dog was Wilford! and we are afraid the world had and still has many like him—by disposition he was generous and daring, and would rather have shot himself through the head than done a deliberate and cruel wrong to any one; but, like most who are generous and daring, his passions were too strong for his better judgment—then again, he was young, and singularly handsome, with a gallant recklessness of manner which lent a dangerous charm to his presence and conversation; and, being thus, it is no wonder that the simple girl should have cherished him from the first as the ideal of her dreams of maiden love—no wonder that Wilford, young, passionate, and impulsive, should have been won by her pretty face and graceful figure, and felt somewhat flattered by the love she had not the art to conceal. He was no practised libertine to take a studied advantage of her innocent affection, but there are times when solitude is dangerous to the young and beautiful—the heart begins to dream, and, lost to all save its own passionate instinct, shuts itself unconsciously to the influence of prudence and the fears of what the world will say. Moralists may condemn, and the untempted virtuous may listen and feel shocked exceedingly, still they do listen, and with a strange degree of virtuous interest, when such stories of wickedness are told to them; yet it is the old, old story—very sad, but very true; and so it had been with our hero and pretty little Bessie.

He was touched to the heart by her words, so expressive of a self-sacrificing and devoted affection, and, in return, made a hundred earnest promises of faith and constancy, which, at the time of utterance, he really meant.

Such promises have often been made before, and, alas that it should be so! broken, and their memory cast away at sight of the first bewitching form and beaming face seen and coveted, perhaps, within a day of having left the lady to whom the broken promises were made.

However, let us keep to our tale.

The reappearance of Bessie's respected parent brought their conversation to an abrupt termination. He bore in his hands a couple of bottles, which had not seen the light for many years, and, setting these upon the table, he closed the trap door, and exclaimed—

"There you are, Captain! a drop of such rare stuff as you don't often taste—bring some glasses, Bessie, and then go to your own room; the Captain may have something to talk about."

"Go to the deuce! get the glasses yourself, and let Bessie alone!"

"Well, have your own way," said Long Jack, with a peculiar look of cunning malice in his usually expressionless eye, "have your own way while you can."

The tone in which he said the last word jarred unpleasantly on Wilford's ear.

"While I can!" he repeated, looking curiously at the last speaker, "now what the deuce do you mean by that?"

The landlord's face resumed its habitual look in an instant.

"I don't mean anything, Captain."

"Don't you," said Wilford doubtfully; "now it seemed to me, Mr. John Long, very much as though you had some idea of slightly interfering with that habit which I have of having my own way: of course I was mistaken?"

"In course you were, Captain. How could I interfere with you?"

"That is best known to yourself. I don't wish to think otherwise, because, for little Bessie's sake, I should not like to have to send a bullet through you."

"I should'nt like that myself."

"Don't make unpleasant remarks, then; they have a touch of treachery; and you know the law of our band."

"Which one, Captain?"

"That which gives death to the traitor," said Wilford, with a calm stern significance, which made the other feel slightly uncomfortable.

"You have always found me faithful," he said.

"And always shall, I trust; but, come, pour out the wine."

Long filled three glasses with the sparkling liquid, and, giving one to his fair companion, the youth emptied another.

"A magnificent draught," he said, "rich and mellow as the nectar of the ancients. Come, Bessie, let us have a toast."

The girl raised her glass, which Wilford for the second time had filled, and, looking into his eyes, said—

"Love to the true, and truth to the trusting."

"A pretty sentiment," he said, kissing her, "and one which I shall not forget. Now, my worthy host, let us have one from you."

"The gentleman of the king's highway!" exclaimed Long Jack, emptying his glass like a trooper; "there, Captain, there; toast for you."

"Nearly equal to the last," said the boy. "Let me re-echo both, and add to them this, 'True to the death!' There, my friend, that is a toast for you—the motto of the band, and all who are connected with it."

"Road-side innkeepers included," said the landlord.

"Exactly; have you had any new customers of late?"

"Two last night."

"Of us?"

"No; they looked like reg'lar nobs; drank the best wine, at least the best I gave them. I don't bring this sort out for chance customers."

"Right, old fellow; stick to that. What were they like?"

"One was a young gentlemen, dressed like a lord; spent his cash freely, too. Such a purse he had, Captain; and his jewels would have made your fingers ache."

"And the other?"

"Same style of rig; but middle aged, and careful of his coin."

"Mounted, or on foot?"

"Mounted—horses fit for highwaymen to ride. They seemed in a precious state about something; and the eldest had an ugly cut on his forehead."

"Ha! did you listen to their conversation?"

"Rather—trust me for that," said Long Jack, with the same cunning twinkle in his eye; "I heard just enough to put you in for a nice job."

"That's the style; let's have it."

"They talked about a gentleman with a black horse and a big dog."

"Did they, though; did they say anything particular about him?"

"The one with the cut forehead swore to have revenge; and the young one swore —"

"The same, I suppose?"

"No; he swore he'd have the girl, in spite of the devil himself."

"So they talked about a girl, did they; well, we shall see how far the promise goes as to his having the young lady in question."

"Then you knows them, Captain?"

"Oh yes; I had the pleasure of meeting them last night."

"And it was you as baulked them in their little game?"

"It was. That cut on the brow was mine, too."

"I thought so," said the landlord, in a tone of admiration. "Why, Captain, you ain't afraid of nothing."

"No," laughed the boy: "it is'nt much to fear."

"You'd best be careful, though; they swore to have your life."

"Ha, ha! they must use their swords a little better, then. Was that all you heard?"

"I heard them talk about coming back—to the Grange, I think it was."

"When?"

"To-night, Captain; so there's a chance for you."

"Which I shall take. Here's something for the information. Good night, old boy; adieu, Bessie;" and, throwing a second handful of gold on to the table, he caressed the girl, and left the house.

The Arabian gave a whinny of delight as his noble master leaped into the saddle, and Wolf seconded the sound with a growl.

"Come, old fellow," said Wilford, and, wagging his heavy tail, in a manner which clearly testified the pleasure he felt at the sound of his master's voice, the mastiff followed.

Suddenly he paused.

At the same instant Selim drew up of his own accord.

Wilford knew what they meant, and, bending forward, he listened intently for a moment or two. He heard that which the keener susceptibility of his four-footed companions had heard before—the distant sound of an approaching rider or riders; for as yet he could not tell whether there was one or more.

He did not stop to ascertain.

He stood in the Hammersmith Road, which then was a mere piece of waste ground, with a hedge of thick bushes on either side of the roadway, and a ditch of some width and depth, which was generally kept well filled with a peculiarly soft and sticky mud, for the better accommodation of any unfortunate traveller who might chance to deposit his carcase therein.

The ditch was fast underneath the hedge, and, being on that side which overhung the road, such an incident as that to which we have just alluded was not of unfrequent occurrence, particularly with such individuals as were in the habit of going home somewhat too heavily laden with good liquor, or, on foggy nights, with individuals in general.

It was over this ditch and hedge that Selim went with one clear bound, and landed safely in the meadow behind, the same moment as did Wolf, who had taken the leap with him.

So suddenly did they disappear that, had any one seen them an instant before, they would have doubted the evidence of their own eyesight.

One moment they had been coming down the road, the next they had drawn up and stood motionless together, the next a bound and they were gone.

Meanwhile the sounds came nearer and more distinct, and two horsemen came into view.

They were riding slowly and talking to each other in a low tone.

"It was a cursed failure," said the elder of the two, "and this mark which that infernal meddler set upon my brow would betray me to him if he should chance to be an inmate of the Grange."

"But your hair conceals it," said the other; "does it not?"

"Yes, but an accident might display it; we must risk it, however. I promised to go down to-night in company with you, and not to keep the appointment would have a certain air of suspicion, not that _he_ would ever suspect you or I; but it is best to have no chance."

"Much," replied the other; "besides, I am impatient again, and wish to make a second attempt to win the fair heiress, even though I should again be rejected."

"She might have been yours by this time," rejoined his companion, "past all power to resist or refuse, had it not been for that boy with his skilful sword and iron wrist; I can hold my own in general, but with him I stood no chance."

"Nor I with his dog," said the other; "how the savage brute growled; I thought he would have torn me to pieces."

"So I should imagine; you groaned dismally enough."

He laughed sarcastically as he spoke, and his companion exclaimed in a tone which he intended should be fierce,

"Do you doubt my courage, sir; if so—"

"Well, proceed, if so, what?"

"Why, why, it is not gentlemanly, considering—"

"The heavy obligation I am under to you; finish your sentence my friend, as that finished it for you."

"Well, you must admit I have paid somewhat heavily for the bare chance of calling the fair Alice mine; my purse is always at your service—"

"And mine."

Both the horsemen drew back with a wild cry of terror.

As the last word left the lips of the younger of the two, a dark shadowy form cleared the hedge with one long bound, and coming from the field alighted silently in the very centre of the road.

Directly in front of the two horsemen.

It was in truth a spectacle to chill the blood, and make the heart grow cold.

A form—a black mysterious awful form—sitting like a centaur on a sable steed.

A steed, black, from head to foot, save for a white star gleaming out from the forehead, and another on the breast.

Then the rider!

A silent nameless figure; a weird demoniac object; a thing created by nature as in horrible mockery of her own beauty, as worked out in human shape; a sight upon which the eye dared not gaze, yet was in spell-bound terror forced to keep intent its startled sense, even while the brain reeled and the soul thrilled with fear.

Seen by the moon's pale glimmer this fearful creature took an aspect more wild and strange even than it was.

Shaped like a man; its limbs were like the limbs of a young Appollo, dressed in the handsome costume of the period; its body was perfect in proportion, sinewy and lithe; its hands were small in size, and like a wolf's hairy paws, with fingers cleft from the centre, and with strong claw-like talons in place of nails.

But the head!

That was the most hideous of all.

The head of a monster—a monster of such a race as may exist in some world yet unknown; a thing like the creation of some appalling nightmare, from which every waking sense shudderingly recoils.

A face—a human face—brute-like and wolfish in every lineament; hairy and black; a savage and repulsive something to which no name could be given.

The eyes were red!

A bright vivid red, gleaming out like living coals from the shaggy brows; beautiful in their dense glowing colour, but cruel in their look as the orbs of a fiend let loose upon the earth.

Such was the thing which faced the stricken sight of the horsemen.

One was a bold man—a man with no pity in his heart, or fear of human peril; but he could not stand before such a spectacle unmoved.

He had laughed to scorn the tale of its existence.

But he saw it now: there standing right before him.

Underneath the monster's horse stood a large black dog—a noble-looking animal enough, but taking a ghastly horror from the presence of its master. Its

THE DUEL IN THE GAMING-ROOM.

eyes seemed to give a pale blue light from out the deep shadow cast by the sable steed.

And with that horse there was a mystery more strange than all the rest.

The sound of its hoofs was never heard.

Even in the leap it had just taken from the meadow over the hedge, and right into the centre of the road, it had come down silent as a shadow.

Since that rider, horse, and dog had stood silent and motionless as stone, the words " and mine " were spoken as the leap was taken.

The horsemen knew what it was they saw.

" Black Wolf."

The words were spoken in a whispered gasp by the elder of the two.

His companion sat with quivering limbs and chattering teeth.

The very steeds on which they sat trembled as

though they knew that they were in the presence of something not of heaven or of earth.

" Black Wolf."

This time the words were spoken by the strange creature, spoken in a deep distinct voice with a clear metallic cold articulation.

Then came a mocking laugh.

An exultant laugh of savage sarcasm, as though the monster took a cruel delight in the terror he created.

" Your money."

With hands that trembled like aspen leaves the horsemen held their purses out.

Both shuddered as that hairy paw touched their fingers.

Black Wolf put the purses in the pocket of his riding coat.

" Your jewels."

One by one they drew their rings from their fingers, then the diamond studs from their wrists and shirt fronts.

Again that hairy paw touched their hands, and the jewels went after the purses.

"Your watches."

They were given to him.

Then he turned to the elder of the two.

"That golden snuff box, set with diamonds."

The horseman hesitated.

Only for a moment.

The words were repeated, and a long slender pistol barrel was levelled in a line with his head.

Reluctantly he drew the costly box from his vest and dropped it into the paw.

Black Wolf turned to the other.

"That miniature in the golden case, set with brilliants, gems, and stars of crystal."

The young horseman gave a dismal howl.

The pistol changed its line, and the hollow tube met his eyes in a way strongly suggestive of perforated foreheads and shattered brains.

His hand shook as though palsied when he held the miniature out to the merciless depredator.

"You are nervous," laughed Black Wolf, as he caught the other's hand in his paws; "you cannot keep it steady."

His victim howled with terror and pain beneath the vice-like pressure; while his hand was still held thus his companion put his hand into his breast, then like lightening he drew a pistol out and fired point blank at the monster's heart.

Black Wolf was not a yard distant from the muzzle of the weapon.

He staggered and dropped the hand he held and put his own paw to his breast.

"A good shot," he said, with his wild mocking laugh, "but I do not want the bullet."

He raised his arm, and the man who had fired felt something strike him in the face, and as it fell he caught it.

It was the bullet which had just left his pistol.

"Horror!" he exclaimed; and expecting instant death for his temerity he covered his face with his hands and cowered down to his horse's neck.

His companion immediately on being released from the monster's grip had slid from the saddle and now crouched on his hands and knees underneath his horse.

Black Wolf's dog evidently looked upon this attitude as one peculiarly his own, and, to the extreme terror of the croucher, he wagged his tail, licked his huge jaws, and advanced towards him.

The dismounted individual was in the saddle the next instant.

There, trembling, he waited in expectation of seeing his companion die for having tried to shoot Black Wolf.

But savage as he seemed the monster shed no blood.

"Go," he said, "on to your destination; attempt to follow one step in my track, or speak of this within one hour from this time, and as surely as you do so, I will rend you limb from limb and throw your dismembered corse to my dog."

He moved aside to let them pass.

His injunction was scarcely necessary, they had seen enough of him for once and had no wish to follow in his track, both struck their spurs deeply into their horses flanks and rode rapidly away.

They had not proceeded five hundred yards when that mocking laugh rang out again, and thinking that he might be in pursuit both turned to look.

The echoes of that sardonic cry of exultation were yet quivering in the air, but the dog, the silent horse, and the wild highwayman were gone.

Gone, like the dark phantoms of a dream at night, gone as they had come, shadow-like, mysterious, and horrible.

---

## CHAPTER IV.

### THE BRETHREN OF THE FIVE STARS.

#### *A Game at Dice—A Wager—And a Duel.*

TEN minutes after the parting between the travellers and Black Wolf, Wilford Leander was riding down the road with the mastiff at his usual place, by the side of Selim.

A strange smile was playing round Wilford's lips, and he muttered to himself.

"A splendid booty altogether, I don't think that my friends of this evening's and to-night's acquaintance will forget this meeting for some time."

He was right those who met him *sometimes*, did not soon forget him. Wilford Leander was not always seen in his present guise, that of the gallant dashing young knight of the road.

For a period of twelve months he had set the law at defiance and baffled every attempt made by the Bow Street officers to effect his capture.

When they were on his track he would keep himself in sight of his pursuers for miles, turning round occasionally to knock the nearest off his horse, then, when nearly overtaken, he had but to put Selim to his speed, and the officers might say good night to him till the next time they met.

It was a difficult matter then to identify him.

He never looked twice alike.

He would stop and plunder a traveller on the King's Highway with the utmost sang froid, and the next hour would make his victims' acquaintance with the grace of a courtier, and with no trace of his former resemblance left.

We have many stranger and more daring exploits to relate.

For the present we will go with him to London.

The strange demeanour of the worthy landlord of the Shepherd and his dog kept recurring to his thoughts with unpleasant persistence.

He knew that Long Jack was faithful to the bond, but he also knew that he was cunning and vindictive in all things concerning himself.

"He would betray me without scruple if he suspected," muttered Wilford.

"I must be on my guard for I did not like his style at all to-night, for the sake of pretty Bessie I shouldn't like to have to shoot him, but faith must be kept, and he knows the penalty, some people would look upon it as a sort of retribution, I have what they call betrayed his daughter, he perhaps suspects and would betray me, what the deuce does it matter to such an old brute as that. I really believe that he has such shocking bad taste that he would rather see her tied in lawful wedlock, sweet arrangement, to some clod-hopping clown, who would look upon her as one of the necessaries of his life, somebody to get his meals ready, when he returns from his honest toil, with the appetite of a glutton, and other attributes in keeping, bah! she was not made for such a fate as that, Love's own temple never held a more bewitching minister, a tempting little sinner, whose beauty makes the sin and brings its own absolution. St. Anthony will never get me for a disciple, I believe he was nothing but an old impostor, like St. Ambrose and Joseph the immaculate, aye, old fellow, what do you say?"

Wolf wagged his tail and shewed his teeth like a wicked dog who fully concurred in the opinion of his wicked master.

A touch to the Arabian and the noble creature bounded on with that peculiar long sweeping stride which was at once rapid and graceful, and half an hour's ride brought Wilford into the heart of London.

He drew up at the door of an old stately house in Jermyn Street, and as he alighted Black Wolf took Selim's rein as before, and watched his master to the door.

Wilford knocked.

The door was opened by a livery servant, richly dressed, who stood silently awaiting for the others to speak.

"Lord Nightshade?" said Wilford, who, as the door opened, had covered his face with a black mask.

"At home," was the reply.

The boy dropped a sovereign into the servant's hand, and ascended the stairs.

Having reached the first landing he paused, and knocked at a door which stood opposite the staircase.

"Enter," said a voice.

He opened the door and stood within the room.

A gentleman, masked and dressed in black from head to foot, stood before him.

"Are the five stars bright?" said Wilford.

"Still bright," was the brief reply, "pass!"

The boy crossed the room, and, putting aside the heavy hangings of crimson velvet, with which the walls were hidden, knocked at a door opposite the one by which he had entered.

A single note was struck upon a bell, and the door opened.

A third gentleman, masked and dressed like the others, confronted him.

"Who comes to the den of the Brethren of the Five Stars?" asked the mask.

"A night guardian of the king's highway!"

"Where is the captain of the band?"

"I am here!"

The masked gentleman drew back and bowed; the bell again sounded, and the heavy hangings which reached from floor to ceiling just behind the masked gentleman were drawn aside, and a startling scene was presented to Wilford's gaze.

A long and lofty room, thickly carpeted and luxuriously furnished, and lit by innumerable waxen tapers at the side, while from the ceiling hung two large and elaborately-worked chandeliers of cut crystals.

Piles of cushions and massive soft couches were arranged around the walls, which, like the rest of the rooms through which he had passed, were hung with crimson velvet, while in the centre stood a large table, surrounded by a circular ottoman, thickly cushioned and padded up the backs.

The table was well laden with wine and other drinks—flanked by a profusion of every delicacy in season, or to be procured by artificial means.

Around this table twenty-four men were seated.

Each of these men had covered his face with a black mask, as they heard the least sound of the bell; but when Wilford spoke the words "I am here," the masks were cast aside, and all sprang to their feet with welcome shouts and outstretched hands.

"Gentlemen," said Wilford, laughingly, "permit me to greet my brothers, and imagine that I have given a similar greeting to each and every one."

A hearty laugh followed this suggestion, and the boy said—

"Twenty-four such grips as I should get would leave a strong and feeling recollection behind them! The last time I trusted my hand into Dick Massey's mammoth fist they got such an awful crush that I could not take straight aim for a week!"

"Ha! ha!" laughed Dick Massey, in a voice like distant thunder, "why, you're the only one in the band whose grip can equal mine, except for the president!"

The president was Captain Rolfe, Wilford's reputed brother.

He sat in a handsome chair, raised slightly from the level of the circular seat; Dick Massey sat on his left, and on his right a place had been left vacant for Wilford, which that young gentleman now took.

It was a strange old house, this den of the Brethren of the Five Stars; access was, as we have seen, easily gained by the initiated, but woe to the stranger or the spy who tried to effect an entrance!

Once having gained an entrance he was a doomed man!

He might see and hear much, and depart apparently unnoticed and undetected; but as surely as he went forth with that fatal knowledge in his keeping, he would be tracked by a member of the band—tracked by a member of that band who were as silent as shadows in their work of death, keen and untiring as the bloodhound in following their prey, and like bloodhound, they would bring him down, and have him dead, with an iron dagger in his heart!

No mercy for the spy or the traitor!

Such was the law of the band.

Let us explain who and what were these twenty-five men who now sat around the table.

A strange set they were as they sat, and in the many faces an artist would have found a complete study of the phases (couldn't help the pun) of human nature.

In some it was the mere brute courage of the bull-dog, in others the recklessness of desperation, and again in others the cool inherent fearlessness of the man who might have been a hero in the days of chivalry, but who, by adverse destiny, had been driven to be what they were now—gentlemen of the road—Highwaymen!

Of the last description were Wilford, Captain Rolfe, Dick Massey, and one or two others with whom in our present story we have no interest.

Of the first, the coarse type of brute courage, was one in particular, one man known as Tiger Blue, a savage-looking ruffian, in whose ferocious aspect might be traced all the worst passions that ever disgraced a being in the shape of man.

Of him we have more to say hereafter.

All were richly dressed, each man according to his own taste, and, taken as a whole, they formed a brilliant company.

These twenty-five men formed the central band of the Brethren of the Five Stars.

The association was formed on a clear and well-regulated principle.

They were of five companies, each of twenty-five, governed by a captain, and with one president, who had absolute sway over all.

His was the master hand, which had drawn them together in one band of unity, which had enabled them to set the laws at defiance.

They had a general fund, into which each man paid a certain sum one day in every week.

Out of the bank thus formed were paid all the outside expenses.

Captain Rolfe knew the power of gold, even with men of high repute, and, while the men were faithful to each other, each one was safe.

The president was in league with the keeper of every prison in the kingdom.

If a man was captured, even tried and condemned, he was sure to escape in some mysterious way.

Then, again, they were in league with the most celebrated jewellers in London, who bought all such plunder as was not inquired after by the loser.

Sometimes a large reward was offered for the restitution of a jewel, a ring, or a trinket—an heirloom, perhaps—or a gift from some dear friend.

In that case application was made at Bow Street, and the affair put in the hands of John Hartley, the most skilful and celebrated of the officers.

He was the only man who could obtain repossession of the article, and the means by which he did so he kept a profound secret.

He was a clever man, and knew that his power to do this gave him a position which he could not well afford to lose.

The secret of his power was a simple one.

Everything, save for actual money, was given into the care of the president, by him to be sold, or restored to the loser.

He had an understanding with John Hartley, by which the article could be restored on payment of a certain sum, if adequate in value to the thing required.

They dealt fairly with each other.

John Hartley kept good faith with Captain Rolfe, for the sake of his own interest as well as for the safety of his life.

More than one of his brother officers had tried to solve the mystery, but they had never lived to report progress.

So, after a time, John Hartley had the business to himself; for, finding that neither threats nor bribes would induce him to disclose the manner in which he recovered the articles, the authorities thought best to let him alone. Besides, they derived a tolerable revenue by the system; and no man is incorruptible.

The same system of laws and regulations applied to each of the five companies, four of which were distributed throughout the country, the one now gathered together being the central band, of which Wilford Leander was captain.

Their operations were confined exclusively to London and its near vicinities.

The house in Jermyn Street, in which they held meetings, was the property of Lord Nightshade, a dissolute nobleman, who had still some influence at court, and kept a splendid establishment, though he had long since run through his inheritance.

The house had two entrances.

One was devoted to the use of the knights of the road, and in their part of the mansion no stranger dared intrude.

The place had been chosen by Captain Rolfe, who in former years had been one of his lordship's chosen friends.

They were faithful to each other still, and, for the sake of their friendship as well as for his own interest, Lord Nightshade let him the place as a rendezvous for himself and companions.

No one ever suspected the nature of this portion of his lordship's visitors.

He had many besides these, who always came in by the other entrance—came in to risk honour and fortune on that curse of high society—gambling.

A splendid suite of apartments were devoted to this maddening pursuit, and there, night after night, the élite of the fashionable world were gathered.

Gentlemen, peers, even princes of the royal blood, went there to play and risk immense sums on the turn of a card or the rattle of the dice.

The gaming rooms communicated by a staircase and passage with the rooms in which the knights of the road held their weekly meetings; of these last only two knew of the existence of the gambling table, and those two only were permitted to enter.

The rest, having met and settled their affairs, always dispersed and went again to their dangerous pursuit.

The two who could remain were Captain Rolfe and Wilford.

To them and their companions we now return.

Captain Rolfe held a written paper in his hand.

On that paper was recorded a list of all the robberies which had taken place since they last met.

The names of the plundered, and the places where they had been stopped, were recorded too.

Captain Rolfe read one by one the particulars of each affair, and as he read the articles were handed over to him by the respective gentlemen who had been engaged in each pleasant and remunerative operation.

"Tiger Blue," he said.

"Here."

Captain Rolfe continued—

"Stopped the Duke of Westland on Finchley Road last Thursday; heavy purse, gold watch and seals, diamond pin, ditto brooch with portrait, two rings, one with large ruby, other with diamonds and opal, and the golden hilt of the duke's sword."

He watched Tiger's face closely as he enumerated each article.

"All right," said Tiger, "except the brooch: I didn't have no brooch."

"Don't lie, Tiger; the duke wants that brooch, and will give a thousand pounds for it."

"I can't help it," said Tiger; "I ain't got it."

"What have you done with it?"

"I never had it," said Tiger, sullenly.

"Lies; you sold it for fifty pounds to an old jew fence: you were a fool, for your share would have been two hundred and fifty. You broke our law, which says that everything should be brought to me, and for that you will forfeit all the rest you have taken."

"I tell you, Captain, I didn't have no brooch."

Captain Rolfe answered him with a smile of scorn.

"You are a bad man," said he, sternly, "a cruel, brutal wretch, totally unfit to sit in company with gentlemen; you are a savage monster, unfit to live—a disgrace to your profession; and not only have you forfeited your share of the spoil by telling a lie and doing a dishonest act unto your brethren, but you have forfeited your life."

"My life!"

Tiger sprang to his feet, and put his hand into his breast.

He glared savagely at Captain Rolfe, who sat regarding him with a look of cold sternness.

The rest looked on, silent and stern as this chief.

The time had not yet come for them to interfere.

"Your life," repeated Captain Rolfe. "There is blood upon your head."

"Blood!" echoed the rest.

"Murder! a cold-blooded, cruel murder. It was a coward cruel deed to outrage and to kill that poor girl in the little cottage at Finchley. You are an inhuman wretch, Tiger Blue, not fit to live, and too base to die by the hand of a brave man."

Tiger stood watching furtively every move made by his companions—watching in deadly fear and wild ferocity, dreading for his own life, and ready to send a bullet through the president on the instant that he spoke the word which doomed him to the death he justly merited.

"We shed no blood except in self-defence," continued Captain Rolfe. "We are sworn to protect the innocent and weak, to help the poor, and to rob the rich, and battle with the strong alone. You, Tiger Blue, have done a deed of savage wantonness, a deed for which the penalty is death."

"Death!" said the rest, one and all, as they rose; "a traitor and a coward! let him die!"

Tiger sprang back with a savage execration, and drew a pistol from his breast.

He took aim at Captain Rolfe, but before he could fire the weapon was dashed from his hand, his arms pinioned, and held helpless in the grip of two strong men.

There was but little hope for him now.

They might shoot him dead, brain, or strangle him, and no sound or cry would pass those thickly-padded walls.

But such was not Captain Rolfe's intention.

He could doom the ruffian to a death as sure—slower in its coming—but as sure to come as the Day of Judgment!

And he did so.

"Let him go," he said.

Tiger's captors released him.

"Now," said Captain Rolfe, "go forth from this time, and for ever you are an outcast from the band, and the hand of every man shall be raised against you! the officers are on your track, and you will be hunted down, but no step will be taken to keep you from the gibbet. You are a doomed man, Tiger Blue! as surely as you killed, pitilessly killed that poor helpless girl. Go! but before you go you shall bear the mark of the outcast and murderer, a mark by which men shall know and shun you as they would a second Cain. Bring him here."

Again the wretch was seized and dragged forward.

"Open his right hand,"

Tiger's captors forced his hand open and laid it on the table, with the palm upwards.

Captain Rolfe drew an iron dagger from his breast. With the point of this he marked a deep cross in Tiger's hand.

The ruffian shrieked for mercy, but his cries fell on hearts, to him, as hearts of stone.

A small vial containing a colourless liquid was then brought, and some of the contents was rubbed into the bleeding wound.

That wound would soon heal, but a red livid cross would remain, a mark beyond the skill of human surgery to efface or hide.

He was now marked with a mark which would go with him to the grave, and now they set him free.

Rendered reckless and desperate by pain he turned fiercely to the president—

"I'll have revenge!" he shouted, "I will, by hell! see if some of your cussed carcases don't swing on a gibbet before long."

And shaking his left hand at Captain Rolfe and his companions, he left the room and reached the street.

He saw Selim and the mastiff at the door, and his first idea was to mount the Arabian and ride away; but a look at Wolf's teeth caused him to alter his mind, and, muttering dark savage threats against all his late associates, he walked away.

"Were you wise in allowing him to go?" asked Wilford.

Captain Rolfe smiled.

"He will not go far," he said, "John Hartley is after him for the murder, and now that he is left to himself he will not escape."

"Not for long," said Dick Massey, a fine handsome fellow, with the face and form of an Achilles, "when a man is cast out of the band, and Jack Hartley is after him, it is a sure case of rope and gibbet."

"So let it be with him," said Captain Rolfe, "he deserves no better fate."

The rest of the men gave up their plunder, and, after an hour or so spent in congenial conversation over the wine cup, the band dispersed, leaving Wilford and Captain Rolfe behind.

Massey was the last to go.

"Which road do you take, Dick?" asked Wilford.

"Dulwich," was the answer; "there's a fat old gent going home with a pretty little wife; I shall frighten the old buffer to death, and persuade the lady to elope with me."

"That's kind," laughed Wilford, "success to your intention."

"The same to you," replied Dick, "but be careful, my boy; don't let the women know too much: you know the proverb 'angels in love, devils being angered.'"

"But I never anger them."

"All right, swear to that; you are never inconstant! youth never is!"

"You are always constant!"

"I—of course I am."

"And could produce fifty fair witnesses to swear to that," laughed Wilford, "never fear, Massey, I am not deeply involved as yet."

"Keep so, then, if you can—good night, captain; good night, Wilford," and Dick Massey went out, with the full intention of keeping his word regarding the old gentleman and his pretty wife.

"You will stay with me to-night?" said Captain Rolfe to Wilford.

"Till to-morrow," was the answer. "I have to tell you an adventure—by the way, I have left Selim at the door with Wolf! just send a person to look after them."

A groom was sent, and the Arabian and his friend, the mastiff, were taken to the stable.

"Shall we risk a hundred or so with the ivories?" asked Rolfe.

"As you please."

"Come, then; we may see a good chance of 'stand and deliver.'"

"Consolatory, that, to any fortunate winner!"

"Bah!" said Rolfe, "it is worse to plunder a man at the gaming table than to stop him on the road."

So saying he led the way through the three rooms by which Wilford had entered, and ascended the staircase which led to that part of the house in which the gamblers were assembled.

Lord Nightshade welcomed them as though they had only just entered the house.

For the most part the gamesters were men of fortune, others ruined spendthrifts on the look out for the young and reckless gallants, many of whom they picked up and introduced to this den of fashion, or there to lead them into the terrible fascination of the game—a fascination which ended in utter ruin.

Some here were sharpers—men upon town—who choose rather to live by their wits than obtain honest employ, or venture into the dangers of a life on the highway.

Such men as these were rigorously excluded if known; but, as in all such places, they contrived to obtain access by some means or other.

The players were gathered in groups varying in number from two to a dozen, round many tables, on which piles of gold and notes were scattered heedlessly, and taken from or added to according as the players won or lost.

Fair play was strictly enforced; any attempt at cheating being summarily punished in any manner, from being kicked down stairs to being pinked with the points of a dozen or two of swords, or pitched out of window.

The last was the most popular mode of dealing with a blackleg.

Wilford and his companion watched the players with curious interest.

Two players in particular attracted their attention.

One was a young handsome fellow, with a pale intellectual face and dreamy eyes, rendered haggard now by desperation.

His companion was a man of about the middle age, with a fierce hardened face, and his bloodshot eyes were fired as with exultation.

He was winning largely.

He rattled the dice and turned them out with the dexterity of an old hand, and at almost every throw he won the stakes.

Wilford watched his play intently.

He had a quick eye, and dexterously as the gambler played he detected something of which he took particular notice.

"Your luck is out, Mr. Danton," said the gambler, "three, four, four; a bad throw that."

He took his throw and turned up two sixes and a five.

"I am singularly fortunate to-night," he said as he pocketed the stakes, "but such luck cannot last, try again, you cannot always lose."

"I have nothing more to lose," said the other with a groan of despair, "I am ruined."

The other laughed.

"Pshaw," he said; "why I have not won above two thousand."

"It was all I had," exclaimed Danton, as he rose and staggered to another seat; "God help me now, for I am lost."

"Never say die," said his late opponent; "I would lend you some of what I've won, but I happen to owe just a couple of thousand."

Wilford looked at the speaker with a sneer, then turned to Danton, and took him aside.

"You have been unfortunate," he said kindly; "I heard the amount of your loss, let me lend you the money."

Danton looked at him in surprise.

"A stranger," he said, "and would you trust me with such a sum."

"Why not? it is not much to me; to you it may be of serious importance."

"It is indeed," said Danton, as Wilford put the

notes into his hand; "God bless you, this generous act has saved me from the worst; yet I know not how to repay you."

"By a promise—a simple one."

"Name it, and by all I hold most sacred I swear to keep it."

Wilford had drawn him to a remote part of the room out of earshot of the players, and he said.

"It is that you never enter a gaming room again."

"I swear it," cried Danton, wringing the generous youth's hand gratefully; "I have been sinful, base, for I have risked that which was not mine own, but from this time I will never set foot in this accursed den; rest assured that I shall well repay you this. It is life to me—hope—a chance to once again be a man; and by the heaven above I will not do such wrong to your generous heart as to ever lend myself again to shame and dishonour."

Wilford pressed his hand, and with a grateful heart young Danton left the house.

"You have done well," said Captain Rolfe, as Wilford returned to him; "I know young Danton well, and partly suspect the purpose of his late opponent."

"His purpose!"

"Yes; young Danton has lately married a girl to whom this man with whom he has just played, Sir Hector Warren as he calls himself, once paid his addresses; persecuted her with dishonourable intent; she repulsed him with the scorn he deserved, and shortly afterwards married Charles Danton. Sir Hector made his acquaintance, and gradually enticed him here; the result you have seen; but for you Danton would have been utterly ruined, and if I mistake not Sir Hector would have urged him to still greater dishonour—the dishonour of his wife—in return for some part of the fortune lost to him by young Danton."

"The scoundrel!" exclaimed Wilford. "a plot worthy of a fiend; see Rolfe, how I will serve him out for this."

So saying, he approached the table where Sir Hector sat counting his nefarious gains, and unconscious of the manner in which Wilford had aided his intended victim to escape his toils.

Seating himself opposite the gambler, Wilford said—

"What say you, Sir Hector Warren, will you stake a fifty on a throw?"

"I am always ready to tempt fortune," replied Warren, who thought the youth was simple enough to be cheated with impunity, "take your throw."

In the game as played then each player had a separate box and set of dice.

Wilford threw.

"Three sixes."

Sir Hector stared.

He could not very well beat that, but he threw and Wilford won.

They threw again, and with the same result; for whatever number Sir Hector made, the boy was sure to beat him.

Warren got excited as his losses increased rapidly.

"Stake higher," said Wilford, "luck may change."

The stakes were increased to two hundred pounds. Still Sir Hector lost.

Lost the two thousand he had won from Danton, and nearly as much of his own.

Was it merely the result of an extraordinary run of good fortune, or had he met with one more skilful than himself.

He grew desperate and reckless at last.

"Five thousand!" cried Wilford, as again he won; "Sir Hector, fortune frowns upon you: will you desist, or have revenge?"

"Revenge!" replied Warren, "win or lose against the five thousand."

"As you please, but it is a heavy sum!"

"I have not lost it yet."

"Throw then!"

Sir Hector rattled the dice, and brought them down upon the table.

By this time a crowd of idlers had gathered round, and stood looking curiously on at the two players, the one an expert gambler, now flushed and excited, the other a mere boy. cool and careless as to whether he won or lost.

Sir Hector raised the cup,

"Two sixes five!" he said triumphantly.

Wilford smiled and brought his cup down.

"Three sixes!" he said as he raised it, "Ten thousand pounds Sir Hector!"

"This is trickery," said Sir Hector red with passion, "curse you I will not pay!"

"Will you not?" said Wilford calmly, while Captain Rolfe kept a watchful eye on Sir Hector's movements; "well, we shall see; there is trickery, Sir Hector, base dishonourable trickery, but it is on your part, cheat, blackleg, and scoundrel as you are; you see I have thrown best, *although I have not played with cogged dice!*"

With a savage cry Sir Hector drew his sword and made a swift pass at the fearless boy.

But Wilford was on his guard.

He had kept his eye fixed on Sir Hector's, and as the thrust came his own weapon flashed out and Warren's went spinning from his hand. "You move very quick, my friend," said Wilford coolly, "but not quite quick enough. Gentlemen, I have called him a cheat and a scoundrel. In company like this, where honour is the rule, such words should not be lightly spoken: I can prove them—see!"

He took up Sir Hector's dice one by one, and struck them each a quick smart blow with his sword.

A murmur of execration broke from the company.

The dice were hollow, the cavity being filled with lead.

"Now, gentlemen," said Wilford, "he says he will not pay. When a man tries to win by cheating, and in spite of that is beaten by skilful, fair throwing, what should be done to him?"

"Turn him upside down," suggested one.

"Agreed—agreed."

"Toss him in the table cloth," said another.

"Do both," said a young nobleman, whose worst fault was the dissipated life he led; "do both; then pitch him out of window."

"Let us carry out the first suggestion, to begin with," said Captain Rolfe.

With a shout, half a dozen of the company rushed upon the luckless cheat, and, in spite of his wild threats and desperate struggles, seized him by the legs, turned him head downwards, and shook him.

All the money he had about him, nearly fourteen thousand pounds, in notes and gold, fell from his pockets to the floor, together with the dice he should have used, but which he had concealed, in order that he might substitute his own.

The baffled and exposed gamester was then set upon his feet, and all that remained of his money, after the ten thousand had been counted out and given to Wilford, was thrust back into his pockets.

Directly he was released he sprang to where his sword lay, and eyed the company with a look of deadly fury.

"Cowards!" he shouted; "come on one by one, and defend yourselves, if you dare!"

A dozen swords were out in an instant, ready to answer him, but Wilford interposed—

"Leave him to me," he said; and the rest instinctively drew back, as the youth confronted Sir Hector, sword in hand.

He looked the very picture of heroic beauty as he stood in graceful attitude, his chest thrown out and his head set back, his left arm raised, and a magnificent diamond ring flashing on the slender fingers of his small white hand. He held the jewelled hilt of his glittering sword in a firm grip, yet not so tightly as to mar the play of his supple wrist, and, from the instant that the weapons crossed, the spectators could so that the elder stronger man would have enough to do to guard himself from the skill of his young antagonist.

Wilford kept his flashing eye fixed intently on the firm bloodshot orb of his opponent, who, excited by the disgrace and humiliation to which he had been subjected, put forth all his strength and skill, and tried every move by which he might take the boy off his guard.

Captain Rolfe looked with proud affection on the gallant youth. He had no fear as to the issue, for he himself had taught Wilford his first lesson with the sword, and since that time he had seen that the pupil was equal to the master; and not the most renowned duellist of the period would have cared to cope with Captain Rolfe Leander.

Sir Hector pressed hard upon his adversary—thrust, lunged, and made every point he could; once he made a lunge with such fearful force that all the lookers on thought to see the dauntless boy impaled; but Wilford saw it coming; a sudden light kindled in his eye; he caught Sir Hector's weapon as it came, kept it firmly down, then gave a swift circular turn to his own sword, and the next moment Warren's blade was lying on the floor in two pieces, while he himself stood disarmed and helpless, the tears of agony starting to his eyes, and his left hand clasped around the dislocated wrist of the sword arm.

A loud burst of applause followed this splendid feat of swordsmanship, and Wilford exclaimed—

"I would kill you, Sir Hector, if it were not that your black blood would sully the brightness of a weapon never yet drawn save in honour; but you will leave this place dejected and disgraced, known as a blackleg and a cheat, and with the knowledge that Charles Danton has escaped your toils, and that your intents towards himself and another whom I need not name are known. It will also be some time before you can use that wrist of yours, so you will have to play left handed; and now, unless you can use your legs, you will carry with you a strong remembrance of this night's affair, for I now start the proposition that you be kicked down stairs and out of the front door."

"Bravo!" said the young nobleman who had before spoken; "that's the idea; let me begin: I always wear thick boots."

He made a dart after the retreating figure of Sir Hector, who, directly the proposition was mentioned, made for the door, which he reached, opened, passed through, and shut just as his pursuer aimed a kick, which, had it reached its destination, would certainly have taken Sir Hector over the banisters; but it did not; the door shut just in time to receive the upraised foot, which went against it with a crash, and sent the owner flying back with extraordinary velocity.

He fell on his back, and slid along the floor, finally putting his head under a chair, which he overturned on somebody else's foot, and a scene of general confusion arose in consequence.

"That's the idea," he said, as he got up amid the laughter of the rest, and fell into a chair instead of under it, "I didn't kick him, but he rolled all the way down stairs; I heard him howl."

This was ascertained to be the truth, for Sir Hector in his haste had put his foot too far out, missed the top stair, and, as a matter of course, gone to the bottom, his backbone being grazed, and his head bumping all the way.

"Is your lordship hurt?" asked Captain Rolfe, keeping down a smile.

"Hurt! could a fellow go against the door as I did without being hurt? that's the idea."

And Lord Tempest Chester, that being the speaker's name and title, took his boot off to see where his five toes were.

They were all right, but quite benumbed by the shock; and having made himself certain on that point, his lordship carefully reinserted his foot in his boot.

"Tempest," said Viscount Clair, a young aristocratic-looking gentleman, and a faithful friend to the man to whom he spoke, "I just had such a capital thought."

"Don't let it go then, there's a good fellow," said his lordship encouragingly, "What's it like, old boy?"

"Why, you see we're used up here in London; I've won a lot of money, and don't care for any more. There's nothing new in the way of fast life, or anything of that sort, and everything's awfully slow, so I thought we'd have a ride."

"You don't call that a capital thought, do you?"

"I have not done yet; when I say a ride, I mean a hunt."

"That's the idea; but what shall we hunt?"

"You have heard of somebody they call the Boy Highwayman?"

"A fellow with a beautiful black horse and a large dog with a big mouth; I know, go ahead."

"Well, we'll hunt him out; I want to buy his horse."

"All right; I'll buy his dog, but where shall we find him?"

"I can tell you, gentlemen," said Wilford, coming forward, "he is on the Richmond Road every Thursday night; may I ask how much you would think of bidding for his horse?"

"A thousand—I don't mind a thousand," said the viscount.

Wilford laughed.

"I don't think you'll get Selim for a thousand," he said.

"Sell him for a thousand; well, I'll give two."

A warning glance from Captain Rolfe told Wilford of his indiscretion in mentioning the name of his horse, a name which fortunately the viscount had misinterpreted.

"And I'll give a hundred for his dog," exclaimed Lord Chester.

"But he might take your money, and not part with either," said Wilford. "Those who meet him don't often take leave without leaving something behind."

"I was always a match for a highwayman," said Lord Chester, "that is if we have a fair fight for it."

"He always fights fair," said the viscount; "I've heard people say so."

"Come," said Wilford, "I will wager five thousand that you will get neither horse nor dog at any price; and another five that if you meet him you will not escape without delivering your purses."

"Done!" said Lord Chester, "Captain Rolfe shall hold the stakes."

"Done!" said the viscount, "the Captain shall hold mine too."

"Very well," said Captain Rolfe. "I think you will lose, my lord; you too, viscount."

"Do you, well we shall see; now, how shall we arrange?"

"You will ride to the 'Shepherd and His Dog,'" said Wilford, "that, as you know, is on the way; then go out one by one to meet him; and I will meet you an hour afterwards to hear the result."

"And Captain Rolfe shall go with us; will you?" asked the viscount.

"With much pleasure," was the captain's reply; "I should like to see the end of this adventure."

"I shall have his horse," said the viscount; "if he won't sell it, I'll fight him for it."

"That's the idea," said his lordship. "I'll fight him for his dog; you shall go first, Clair, and when you've got his horse tell him to wait for me."

"Of course, that is if he don't run away."

"He never runs away," said Wilford.

"That's settled then," said Chester; "you will be there Captain Rolfe?"

"Without fail; I shall ride down with you."

"And you too, Mr. Leander?"

"I shall be engaged in the evening," said the youth. "I will come to you at the 'Shepherd' by ten o'clock; you will meet him on the road about nine.   This is Wednesday, so it will be to-morrow."

"At nine," said the viscount, "we will be there: you will be sure to come?"

"Gentlemen," said Wilford, as he went out with Captain Rolfe, "I never fail!"

---

## CHAPTER V.

### TIGER BLUE CONCOCTS A PLAN OF VENGEANCE.

BEFORE we relate the result of the adventure between the Boy Highwayman, Lord Tempest Chester, and the Viscount Clair, we have an incident or two to tell concerning other of our characters.

When Tiger Blue, the discarded member of the central band, was turned from the den, as the gentlemen of the road designated their rendezvous, his soul was full of black and bitter thoughts against his late companions.

"I would betray them all," he muttered savagely; "I'd betray the president, but he knows about the Finchley job, and when a cove's red-handed they won't take him as king's evidence, but I'll sell his brother, the boy Wilford; there's a thousand pounds reward for him, and I'll have it, curse 'em.   There ain't no reward for none on the others, but I'll have blood-money for some of 'em."

Blood-money was an allowance of forty pounds, given by the government for the apprehension of any malefactor, such as highwaymen, horse or sheep stealers.

The vindictive ruffian was galled as much by being deprived of his share in the spoil he had taken as by the red cross on his hand, though the acute pain of the wound kept him keenly alive to the fact of its existence.

He proceeded to the office in Bow Street, and without much preliminary conversation stated his intention and ability to lead them to a place where they might capture the celebrated Boy Highwayman, the most renowned and daring of the race.

"Can you?" said one of the officers, "you must be clever then, that's all.   We've been hunting after him for something like twelve months, and haven't got him yet, have we, Butler?"

"Seems like it," said Butler; "the most as ever I got was a bite from his dog; crikey! I thought he'd never let me go."

"It wasn't so bad as the kick his horse gave me," said the other; "it doubled me up, and made me feel sick for a week; I thought I was never coming down."

"You'll catch him if you come with me," said Tiger Blue.

"Where is that?"

"A dozen places, but I know them all."

"Then we'll go to every one."

"And when shall I get the reward?"

"As soon as we get the highwayman."

This was conclusive, and without further word Tiger accompanied them out.

"Shall we go on foot," asked the man called Butler.

"Yes," replied Tiger, "we can't carry a horse about with us."

"No! but the horse might carry us."

"He might; but he'd better not."

This was Tiger's remark, and it elicited a grin, followed by a titter, from Butler, the junior officer, and a snarl from Hunter, senior ditto.

"You mustn't think to take him like a lamb," continued Tiger, "cos you won't; he can fight, and when he's hunted he does fight."

Hunter and his brave coadjutor, Butler, knew it.

"You must collar him unawares or you won't collar him at all."

The officer knew that too.

"The only difficulty," said Hunter, "is that he must be taken alive, or no reward is given, if we might shoot him now."

"Yes," said Butler, "if we might, but we mustn't, and if we did it wouldn't be any good; I've fired enough bullets at him to kill a regiment."

"You," said Hunter, scornfully, "you couldn't hit a haystack."

"You could," replied Butler, scornfully, "but you'd miss anything else."

"When you've done being witty," observed Tiger, "perhaps you'll listen to my plan for trapping him."

Both men became suddenly attentive.

"There's one place he goes to," said Tiger Blue, "the road-side inn at Hammersmith—do you know it?"

"Long Jack's house, the Shepherd and His Dog."

"Yes."

"We know it."

"Well, that will be the most likely place, Long Jack's got a daughter, a pretty little gal, the boy is a devil with the gal, so he's sure to get into mischief there."

"I see," said Hunter, "go on."

"Her father's a queer old stick," resumed Tiger, "and is somehow proud of the gal, it will be an easy job to work on the old man's suspicion, and get him to betray the captain."

"We'll try it anyhow, but it won't do to seem too eager, women are devilish quick in these things, and if the gal smells a rat the game will be up."

"We had better lurk about the neighbourhood," said the traitor, "and watch for him, we may see a chance to take him without letting Long Jack know anything about it."

"Suppose he don't go that way at all," enquired Butler.

"Suppose he don't," said Tiger Blue, "perhaps you know where he will go."

"He mightn't go there."

"Where else then?"

"I don't know, Finchley perhaps," rejoined Butler. Tiger turned pale.

"Finchley," he stammered; "why, why—what makes you think he'd go to Finchley?"

"Who knows, he might as well go there as any other place."

"Finchley," repeated Hunter, reflectively, "fits him, that's where the murder was committed."

"He must have been a brutal wretch whoever did it," said Butler, "I should like to see him swing."

Tiger began to feel uncomfortable.

"You've chosen a pleasant thing to talk about," he said at last, "murder and gibbet, if you ain't got nothing else to say you'd better hold your row."

"We didn't mean to be personal."

"What do you mean?"

"Nothing only you don't seem to like us to say anything about gibbets."

"It hurts his feelings perhaps," said Butler.

"Or his conscience," said the other, "after all it ain't a nice job to sell a pal."

"Ain't it?" said Tiger, savagely, "you'd think different if you'd been served as I have."

"Very likely; what's the boy done to you?"

"What's that to you? I hate the lot!"

"What lot?" asked Hunter, quickly.

"No matter—stick to the business in hand—never mind me or why I do it."

"All right, my friend; it's no affair of ours; all we have to do is to catch him."

"That's all," said Butler.  "I say, Hunter, who's got the Finchley job in hand?"

"Jack Hartley; he said to-night that he'd have the murderer in less than forty-eight hours!"

"He will, too, if he said so," rejoined Butler, "he never speaks till he's sure."

This was consolatory to Tiger Blue, who knew that the man of whom they spoke was like a bloodhound when once put upon the scent.

He felt very much inclined to take to his heels and

BESSIE OVERHEARING THE PLOT TO CAPTURE WILFORD.

leave the officers to capture the highwayman as they best could; but the thought that his first attempt at flight would arouse their suspicions, and perhaps cause them to send a bullet after him, had the effect of altering his mind.

It was a long walk to the neighbourhood of the road-side inn, and little more was said on the way.

Both the officers were disguised, and having reached the "Shepherd," they took a room for the night, pretending to be travellers.

All the next day Tiger Blue waited eagerly for the coming of the youth he intended to betray. His savage longing for revenge overcame his prudence, or he would have known that it was dangerous to stay near the haunts of any of the gang after the warning given by Captain Rolfe.

Hunter and Butler were quite as eager for their prey, but more cautious in their actions; they were **No. 3.**

used to their work, and kept well to their assumed characters.

Tiger Blue was well disguised; but no amount of artifice could conceal the naturally brutish look of his face, and Long Jack's cunning eye detected him at first sight.

"I wonder what his game is?" thought mine host, "and who those coves are as is with him; strike's me he's on the peach; bad game if he is."

The three men were in a room opposite the bar, and Long Jack, ensconced among his mugs and bottles, watched them closely, though apparently quite unobserved.

"Here, landlord!" shouted Tiger, "bring some more lush; we can pay for it."

"So I should think," observed Long Jack, "you seem well up for coin."

"Nothing to what I shall be," exclaimed the

ruffian, "we shall have plenty more soon, shan't we?"

"Perhaps," replied Hunter, who never made sure of anything until he had got it safe.

"And perhaps not," rejoined Butler, who saw that they were in for a difficult task, "we shall know better in a day or two."

"Just as I suspected," thought Long Jack, "Tiger's on the peach, and the other two is laggers; I wonder who they're after?"

"Do you stay long in this part of the country?" he asked aloud.

"It all depends," answered Tiger.

"Sporting, perhaps?" said Long Jack, who felt curious.

"We shall do a little shooting, I daresay."

"Very likely," observed Butler, "is there much game about here?"

"Lots! there's some nice birds in the neighbourhood; but they ain't to be caught with chaff."

"We don't use chaff, my man," said Hunter, "we know the sort of game too well."

"How do you catch them, then?"

"Set a trap."

"Which, perhaps, the bird won't come into; but sometimes when people set traps they put their own foot in it."

Hunter began to think that the worthy landlord was not quite so unsophisticated as he seemed, and thought it might be as well to take him into confidence.

He gave utterance to his first thought in a manner which he intended should be very complimentary

"It strikes me, Long Jack," he said, "that you ain't such a fool as you look."

"Thank you, you're pertickler kind to say so!"

"What do you take us for?"

"Birdcatchers."

"Well, we are, but we only catch a envious sort of bird, such as might be caged in your house occasionally?"

"Night kind, I suppose," said Long Jack, distending his huge mouth like a cod-fish, "you'll find em rather hard to trap!"

"Not with your help!"

"Which, perhaps, you won't get."

"If you are wise we shall."

"Tell us your game then, and what's to be got by it if you want my help; I must know exactly what to do."

"That's the way to speak, we can do business better if we have a good understanding together."

"Much."

"Well, we want the Boy Highwayman."

"Who?" exclaimed Long Jack.

"The Boy Highwayman."

Long Jack indulged in a perilous chuckle.

"Don't you wish you may get him!" he said, laying his finger at the side of his nose, "he! he! he! why don't you try to catch the great Sea Serpent?"

"Because we don't want him," said Tiger Blue, who thought he had said something witty, "we want the Boy Highwayman, and we'll have him too."

"Hold him tight when you do, it ain't a very easy job to hold him even when he's caught."

"We'll manage that," exclaimed Hunter, "now, Long Jack, sit down and let's settle how it's to be done"

The landlord hesitated for a moment.

He knew how dangerous it was to take part in such a thing as the betrayal of any of the band, and that danger was greater still when it was the betrayal of one who was idolized by every one of his brethren.

Long Jack had a hard struggle with his feelings.

Fear, cupidity, and revenge.

He hated the handsome youth now, hated him with all the venom of his malicious nature.

Wilford had seduced his daughter, *and Long John knew it.*

On going for the wine ordered by the boy he had listened to the conversation between the pretty Bessie and her lover.

A singular man by nature was mine host of the Shepherd and his Dog, without a particle of honesty or honour in his heart, and craftily cunning, as in reality he was, the man loved, and was proud of his daughter.

He had been kind to her mother, who loved him well in spite of his want of beauty; and now that she was dead, pretty Bessie was all he had to care for.

It was actually his very ugliness which had made him vicious.

People had served him and made coarse jests at his appearance, and from the time of his birth no living creature had bestowed a kind thought upon him, or given him a kind word;

Except his wife, who had been dead many years.

And from that time he had only cared for Bessie, who, to say the truth, was always affectionate and kind to him.

So when the man found that the child had been wronged, he felt all the malice of his nature rise against her wronger.

He did not stop to think that the girl may have been a willing sacrifice to her own passions.

She was betrayed, and he would have revenge.

He had lain awake all night since he heard the fatal conversation, trying to think of some way by which he might gain his vengeance.

And now he had a chance.

Wilford was coming back that night to the roadside Inn, and there were two officers and a traitor waiting for him.

He could now be betrayed, captured, hanged.

That was revenge—real, true, and deep revenge; death, hanged on the gibbet, where he could go and watch the dying pants of the gallant boy's agony, the brave dashing fellow, who had only sinned through the impulse of his youthful ardent nature.

Long Jack saw all this in anticipation, and as the idea grew strong upon him, he brought his hand down heavily upon the table, and with a fearful oath exclaimed—

"I will do it, curse him, I will by g—d!"

"Will you?" said Tiger Blue, springing to his feet, "then you're the right sort; I hates him, I hates them all, but curse me if I think I hates him like you do!"

Long Jack gave a savage laugh.

"You hate?" he said scornfully, "what is your hate for? you've been kicked out of the gang, I suppose, for some scurvy trick or other, and you want to lag him for the sake of the swag. I want no money; I don't sell him for that; I want revenge—revenge, man, that's what I want."

"You shall have it!" said Hunter, surprised by the savage bitterness of the other's tone, "blessed if you don't look like a hungry bear,"

Tiger Blue looked anything but pleased at the way in which Long Jack had spoke to him; but, in the landlord's present mood, thought it best to say nothing, though he set it down mentally as a grudge to be paid off at some future time.

"When shall we have a chance?" asked Hunter.

"To-night," replied Long Jack.

At that moment Bessie came down stairs, and went quietly into the little room behind the bar.

Her face was very pale, but her lips were set firmly together in a firm determined manner, which was very unusual with her.

She elevated her little hands, and looked intently at the three men that were with her father.

She wanted to know them again.

They had not seen her go into the room, and, unconscious of her close proximity, proceeded to arrange their plan for Wilford's capture.

And Bessie, with white face and bloodless lip, sat listening to every word.

They had laid a skilful plot, as will be seen in our next chapter, but, skilful as it was, and clever as were those who laid it, they were no match for the brave devoted girl *who meant to save her lover in spite of them.*

---

## CHAPTER VI.

HOW THE BOY HIGHWAYMAN WON HIS WAGER WITH THE VISCOUNT AND LORD TEMPEST CHESTER, AND HOW TIGER BLUE, WITH THE OFFICERS, MADE A SLIGHT MISTAKE, AND CAUGHT WHAT THEY DIDN'T WANT.

BESSIE heard the whole arrangement.

The plan did credit to Mr. John Long, who rubbed his hands and chuckled gleefully as he thought of his anticipated vengeance.

Tiger Blue and the officers were to hide in the wine cellar.

The cellar was fitted with a small iron grating, by looking through which any one concealed could see every traveller who passed.

"He'll be along with Bessie," said her father, "in the little room behind the bar; he's sure to send me down for some wine, and that'll be your time; when the trap-door's up you can't see from the room to the bar, except by looking over the top, when you can just see a customer's head, though I don't see a customer's head very often, which is all through that infernal Black Wolf; he terrifies people's hearts out of their carcases, and people is afraid to stay out after dark."

"Ah," said Hunter, "I should like to catch Black Wolf."

"Should you," said Butler, "well, I ain't ambitious; if you like to try you may have all the glory, I'm content to catch the Boy Highwayman."

"You!" said Hunter scornfully, "you're afraid of his very name, because people say he's ugly. I don't believe it; I never saw anything uglier than myself, except when I look at you."

"Which is just my case," retorted Butler; "I like to hear you talk: why, if you or anybody else was to go after him, he'd tear you all into little bits, and give you to that big dog, which people say is just the size of a young donkey."

"Who believes that? I don't."

"Never mind," growled Tiger Blue, "stick to what we've got to do; when you once begin to get witty there's no knowing when you'll stop. Some day you'll both on you get so sharp that you'll cut each other up into little slices. Now, Long Jack, let's have the rest of the plan."

"There's not much more to say; all you've got to do when the trap's up is to come up quietly, and crawl round to the side of the door on your hands and knees; I'll stand in the doorway, so as to hide you, then you can pounce upon and coller him, curse him. I'd poison his wine, only he always makes me drink with him."

Still Bessie sat with the same quiet look on her pretty face; her lips almost white, and her eyes burning with a look of deep determination. She had made up her mind that the officers should *not* capture Wilford, and the resolution only grew stronger in proportion with the difficulties to be overcome.

She rather liked the idea of the officers going into the cellar.

It made her self-imposed task more easy.

They might go down; all she had to do was to take that they did not come up again till they were wanted.

So the plan was arranged, and all the bloodhounds had to do was to wait the coming of their victim.

He would come—of that they felt assured, and were more certain still, when at about nine at night they heard the sound of horses' feet coming down the road.

"Down with you," said Long Jack; "here comes somebody, and perhaps it's him."

He raised the trap-door, and Tiger prepared to descend first.

A ladder was the mode of descent, and Tiger was about half way down, when the trap-door slipped out of Long Jack's hand, and sent the descender down all at once.

"Damn your awkwardness," shouted the bruised individual, "you've nearly broke my neck."

"Very sorry," said Long Jack, "couldn't help it; it slipped."

"Don't let it slip again," said Hunter; "I prefer going down one step at a time."

Which he did—and very carefully, only as he went in the dark he put his foot between two of the bars, lost his hold, and hung down head first.

"Are you all right?" asked Butler.

"Curses, no; I've nearly bit my tongue in two."

"Which would make it ever so much too short," said Tiger as he pulled him out, "now, number three, come along."

Number three came very cautiously, and the trap-door was closed.

"They wouldn't feel quite so comfortable in the dark," thought Long Jack, "if they knew what they'd got close to 'em."

A very queer old house was the "Shepherd and his Dog." It had some very mysterious nooks and corners, and the cellars were the most curious of their kind that wine was kept in.

Long Jack was very rich.

He was then possessed of more money than is generally got by keeping a roadside inn.

Then, again, his trade was not very great.

So it is to be inferred that the few customers he had spent a great deal of money when they came.

Even those who spent most—and they were the gentlemen of the road—could not help wondering how it was that he got so much.

He let them wonder.

Mr. John Long was a very prudent man, and never let anybody know too much.

Some people are so very inquisitive.

And there was one once who was gifted with such an inquiring mind that he slept in the house one night, intending to get up before anybody else did and take a quiet look all about the place.

He was a Bow Street officer! and a very active member of society in his way.

He could not help feeling interrested in Long Jack's peculiar method of conducting business, so he just went down to see how it was done.

He went alone, without telling anyone where he was going, and, having reached the "Shepherd and his Dog," he took a room for the night.

And at about three o'clock in the morning his inquiring mind took him out of bed, led him all over the house, and finally conducted him into the cellars.

Where he lost himself!

But he found something there which made him feel very much as though he had better not have come.

He would have gone away again only for one trifling circumstance.

He could'nt find his way out!

In which predicament he was found by his worthy host, whose mind on that particular night got to be inquiring like his customer's, and thinking, perhaps, he might not be comfortable in his house, Long Jack went to see.

And found that he was not there.

So, thinking that he might have missed his way, he searched till he found him in the cellars.

From whence we may surmise he led the way, for the officer was never seen afterwards.

Long Jack told his daughter that the customer went away very early in the morning, which, perhaps, he did, assisted on his way by the thick end of a very heavy stick, which Long Jack burned in the morning.

It was quite red at the thick end, and looked altogether as though it had gone just a little too far in somebody's skull.

Which, perhaps, it had; but Long Jack never told anybody.

But there was somebody who wanted to know all about it, and, what was more, he fully intended to do so.

This second inquiring gentleman was Mr. John Hartley.

He was one of those men who, whenever they feel at all inquisitive, never rest until they have satisfied their curiosity.

People said that perhaps the officer had stolen something and run away.

John Hartley said that he had been *murdered!*

Then people said "Where is the body?"

Because, when a man is murdered, his body must be somewhere.

An opinion in which John Hartley perfectly agreed.

And he meant to find that body.

But he was full of business just now.

The first thing he intended to do was to catch the man who killed the girl at Finchley.

Then he had another case in hand in which he had been engaged fourteen years.

It was to find out what had become of three people who had disappeared from Wayncliffe Grange.

Two were Lady Wayncliffe and her infant son, the third was Lord Henry Rivers.

For the present we will leave him and return to the "Shepherd and his Dog."

The night was singularly clear, and the three men concealed in the cellar could see every object which passed as they looked through the grating.

They had gone down just as the sound of a horse's hoofs was heard, and got to the grating just in time to see who the rider was.

A young horseman, mounted on a black Arabian, and followed by a black mastiff.

"Wilford Leander."

"The Boy Highwayman."

"That's him," growled Tiger, as the youth rode on.

"The very man," said Hunter.

"So it is," observed Butler.

"Let's tumble up, then, and go after him."

And they would have tumbled up and gone, only when Tiger Blue knocked his head against the trap he found that it was bolted.

"Open the door!" he shouted.

"Hold your row," growled a voice from above, "there's some more people coming."

"But we shall lose the boy!"

"No, you won't."

"He's just rode past!"

"Wait 'till he rides past again, then."

"Curse you for an obstinate ass; he will escape!"

"The same to you; but I know what I'm about."

"Do you intend to let him go?"

"No."

"What then?"

"Wait 'till he comes back."

At this point of the conversation Long Jack moved away, and Hunter pulled Tiger down by the leg.

Three horsemen had drawn rein at the door.

One of them dismounted.

"We shall be back soon," said one of the others, "I know I shall get his horse."

"Very well, viscount, I shall be most happy to give you the stakes."

Tiger Blue knew the speaker's voice.

It was Captain Rolfe.

He had dismounted, and was about to enter the inn.

Then the third one spoke.

"That's the idea; I know I shall win, captain; I shall dismount, too, and wait for Clare. Don't be long, old boy; take his horse, and tell him to wait for me—I want his dog, you know."

"I wish you may get it," thought Captain Rolfe.

"All right," exclaimed the viscount, as he rode off; "I shall come back on the Arabian."

"That's the idea; I'll come back on the big dog."

Lord Tempest dismounted as he spoke, and shouted for the landlord in this style—

"Hallo, 'Shepherd!' you with the bundle of sticks and the ugly chopper, come and take the animals!"

"All right, gentlemen," said Long Jack, "this way."

"The deuce! we don't want to go to the stables!"

"No, sir; in the house, please—little room behind the bar."

"I wonder whether that is the shepherd, or his dog?" said his lordship, as he looked after Long Jack's retreating figure, "what a little monster!"

He followed Captain Rolfe into the room.

Leaving them to their wine, we shall follow Wilford.

When he had rode some distance past the inn he brought Selim to a stand, and listened.

He heard nothing yet.

Then drew a watch from his pocket, and looked at the jewelled dial.

It was just nine o'clock!

"They will not be long," he muttered, "now to make a slight change in my appearance."

First he covered his face with a black mask.

Then he put a heavy black feather in his hat.

And, lastly, he took off his coat.

It was of rich crimson velvet, elaborately embroidered in gold; but by the simple process of turning it inside out, and getting into it again, it was converted into a coat of black velvet, trimmed with braid of the same colour.

This being done, he sat upon his steed in that statue-like motionless manner which had now become habitual to him.

Wolf, as usual, laid down under Selim.

So for a few moments he stood, listening for the sound of those whom he knew would come.

Suddenly the Arabian set his ears forward, and Wolf gave a low growl.

"The viscount!" muttered Wilford, "I hear him now."

His words were correct.

Viscount Clare came down the road at a trot, and as he saw the silent horseman standing in the road, he gave a shout—

"Here you are," he said; "by Jove, I say, I want to buy your horse."

Wilford did not answer.

"Look here, my friend, don't sit there like the commandant waiting for an invocation from the stars; I want to buy your horse."

Still no answer.

The viscount began to feel a sensation of awe creep over him.

It seemed so strange to see those black figures standing there so motionless and still. The rider had not moved hand or foot, and both horse and dog stood as though they had neither life or motion.

"Don't stand there like that!" exclaimed the viscount, pressing forward, "you look as though you had been carved in black marble; but you don't chisel me out of the horse; so now speak, as here goes for a dig."

He drew his sword.

Still the boy moved not.

"Why the devil don't you say something?" exclaimed the viscount, getting more excited, "I want to buy your horse—I've a heavy wager on—I'll give you what you like, only do say something, there's a good fellow."

The silent horseman did.

He drew a long glittering pistol from his belt, and levelled it right at the viscount's head.

Then he said—

"Now, take your choice—let me have your purse, or I will let you have a bullet!"

The viscount did not flinch.

He was a brave fellow, and did not care one jot for the little round hole which was just in a line with his right eye.

"You may fire if you like," he said, "but I cannot return the shot, because I don't carry firearms; but I wear a sword, and, if you like, I'll fight you for it."

Wilford replaced his pistol.

Nothing won upon him so quickly as an act of fearless courage, and he held out his hand.

"You do me honour, Viscount Clair," he said, "and I will fight you for your purse with much pleasure; it is seldom that I meet with one who is at once a gentleman and a man, that I should grieve were I to miss the opportunity of crossing swords with you."

"So should I," exclaimed the viscount, as he took Wilford's hand. "By Jove I like you; I say, how did you know my name?"

"I will tell you at some future time."

"Very well; now look here, I have laid a wager that I shall get your horse—will you part with him?"

"No."

"Not for a thousand?"

"No."

"Two?"

"No."

"Three?"

"No."

"Four?"

"No."

"Five? come, five thousand you know, my dear fellow; just consider—five thousand for a horse!"

"I would not part with him for a dukedom!" said Wilford, "I would slay the man without remorse who would dare to set his foot in Selim's stirrup! but I'll tell you what I'll do."

"By Jove, do!"

"You are, I know, a good swordsman?"

"Just try me! by Jove, I shall have the horse in no time!"

"Well, I will wager Selim against your purse and sword that I disarm you in less than five minutes."

"How? By Jove, I shall get the horse, win the five thousand, and ride home in triumph!"

Wilford smiled as he dismounted.

"Come, viscount," he said, drawing forth his weapon, "Wolf shall be timekeeper; it is twenty minutes past nine; in five minutes this must be decided."

"By Jove, yes, a fair fight, come on."

Wolf took his master's watch in his mouth, and held it so that the clear moonlight fell upon it. Selim went and stood by the side of the viscount's horse, and the two gentlemen faced each other sword in hand.

Both were very young—the viscount was not yet twenty; both were handsome and graceful, and both were masters of the art of fence.

To fence well was then a part of a gentleman's education, for there were times in which an insult was answered by a blow and a swift combat, which usually ended in death on one side or the other.

Duels were frequent then, until the law stepped in and made it a criminal act to draw or wear a sword; it was declared brutal, and the punishment was heavy on any one who dared to disobey.

But this was not until many years after the period of our story.

The sword was then the gentleman's weapon of defence, as in truth it should be now, for a duel fought foot to foot and sword to sword is surely not so brutal as the revolting spectacle of modern times, when two men are allowed to face each other in cold blood, and beat each other's heads into shapeless masses of blood and bruises.

Anyway, it looked a sight fit for the days of chivalry, when Wilford and the viscount stood opposed. Neither meant to do the other hurt, and both were cool and reckless, though a chance thrust or a slip of the foot might have been fatal to either. They placed their weapons as they held them, hilt to point; then each took a step back, and the steel blades met with a cold clash.

"By Jove," said the viscount, as the point of Wilford's sword touched his breast, "that was deuced near."

So near, that had Wilford chosen he could have cleft the other's heart.

But he liked the viscount too well to take advantage of an opening. In fact, once or twice he had to draw his arm back, or the other in his eagerness would have rushed to certain death.

Still the young nobleman could use his weapon in a style which would have soon astonished a less skilful swordsman than the boy with whom he fought. Wilford liked it all the better; he had met somebody whose skill was nearly equal to his own, and he could show now to what he was equal when the occasion required.

"Four minutes, viscount," he exclaimed; "hold your own now, for my Selim is at stake."

"So is my five thousand," said the viscount, "by Jove, that's it—no!"

While speaking so he made a splendid attempt to disarm the boy, and for an instant it seemed as though he had done it, but Wilford only laughed; his hand tightened as he felt the pressure, and he held his sword as in a vice, turning his wrist the while, so as to meet the motion of the opposing weapon; then with a swift stroke he disengaged his sword, and as the other paused, not exactly knowing where to guard, the boy's weapon seemed to twine like a snake around his own, and it had gone from his hand before he could even make his usual exclamation, which was—

"By Jove!"

He said again as Wilford took his watch from the mastiff's mouth, and exclaimed.

"You see, viscount, I have won; it is just the time to a second."

"Then it's all up with my five thousand," said the young nobleman, as he drew out his purse, "here you are, I have lost; what a melancholy object I shall look riding back without my sword."

"Never mind," said Wilford, "you shall have it back again soon."

"I cannot help it if I don't; I lost it fairly, and you won it well; so good night, but don't go away yet, a friend of mine is coming after your dog."

"Let him come, but I cannot wait long, I have an appointment at ten."

"By Jove, so have I; but look here, what are you going to do with my sword?"

"Keep it for a little while."

"Look here, I'll buy it back."

"What! without your money?"

"Money! I've got plenty."

"Rather a dangerous confession, considering that you stand before a knight of the road."

"Yes, but then I have paid my forfeit; we have crossed swords as gentlemen, and whoever you are I shall look upon you as my friend when and wheresoever we may meet again. Fred. Clair is not a fellow to howl over a few thousands; but I should like my sword."

"You shall have it, viscount," exclaimed Wilford, "but as I intend to have your friend's as well, I will return both together; for the rest, I may claim your friendship sooner than you think."

"You shall have it; but, I say, don't forget my sword. Look here, I shall be at the road-side inn, you know, 'The Shepherd and his Dog,' will you bring it there?"

"I will."

"When?"

"At ten o'clock; I trust, of course, to your honour in this."

"I will answer for your safety with my life," exclaimed the viscount, as he rode away. "Look out for your dog, I know you will lose him."

"Shall I have to fight for him?"

"Yes, but Tempest is sure to beat you; he always beats everybody, except me."

"Very well, tell his lordship not to keep me waiting."

"By Jove," thought the viscount, "he knows Chester too. I wonder who the deuce he is; he must be a wonderful fellow: he's going to keep two appointments at ten o'clock, by Jove."

And cogitating thus the viscount rode back to the inn.

"Hullo!" said Tempest, as his friend entered, "where's the horse?"

"Along with your dog, old fellow; my sword is there too, so you may as well bring them all together."

"Ha, ha!" laughed Chester, "that's the idea; so I will."

"Will you though; suppose he gets your sword too?"

"Ah, but he won't," said his lordship, as he mounted his horse, "nobody could ever take my sword."

"By Jove, that's just what I thought, but it went: so did my purse."

"And your five thousand too," said Captain Rolfe.

"I don't care, Chester will lose his; then we shall both be miserable alike. Now, old fellow, go ahead, he's waiting for you down the road, you know."

"All right," said Tempest, as he rode away, "that's the idea; I shall bring back such a lot."

"Ah!" said the viscount, "that's just what I thought."

"I daresay," exclaimed Captain Rolfe; "never mind, viscount, we have just twenty minutes left, and there is just a possibility of his lordship winning his own wager, and your's too."

It was, of course, just possible, but the improbability was something extensive.

When Lord Tempest Chester reached the spot where Wilford stood, he found him still dismounted, while Wolf stood by Selim's side, holding the viscount's sword in his mouth by the hilt.

The sagacious mastiff looked at Chester with a glance, which plainly showed that he was speculating on the extreme likelihood of having his lordship's sword as well.

"Now, my lord," said Wilford, "do not let us lose time; you want my dog, with whom I do not intend to part, unless you are more skilful with your sword than I with mine. Are we to fight?"

"Of course; I have come all the way from London with that particular intention, so come on."

"Do you know the terms of our contest?"

"No; it don't matter, we'll fight, that's the idea. I must have your dog."

"So you shall, but on these terms: I do not want to shed your blood, my lord; our fight is a mere trial of skill, and the stake is, my dog against your purse and sword, that I disarm you within five minutes."

"The deuce! I don't think you can."

"We shall see," said Wilford, as he faced Lord Chester, "that's the idea."

"The deuce! confound it, look here," said Tempest gravely, "don't rob me of my immortal speech, I can stand anything but that."

"I will not do so again," laughed the boy, "it was an act of shameless vandolism, I confess."

"Cruel," said his lordship, as their blades met; "now then."

His lordship was much more cautious in his way of fencing than was the viscount; he did not attempt to disarm his antagonist, only he took particular care that his antagonist should not disarm him.

So far the chances were all on his side, and Wolf began to look as though he did not at all like the prospect of changing masters.

But Wilford knew what to do.

He saw that he had to deal with a man who kept wonderfully cool, and only fenced with the intention of not losing his weapon.

"You see," said Tempest quietly, "it's all fair, Iv'e only got to stick to my sword for five minutes, and

you can do as you like with yours. I think I shall have the dog—what a fine fellow he is."

He left off speaking suddenly, and became more watchful.

He saw that the boy's eyes gleamed with a steel-like glitter, and that a smile was deepening around his lips.

"Now, my lord," he exclaimed, "guard!"

He made a sudden pass, with his wrist raised on a level with his shoulder, and Tempest was scarcely in time to parry.

Wilford's blade pressed tightly on the others, and his lordship tried in vain to disengage.

"It's going," he thought, as he felt the hilt slowly being forced from his fingers, "if I could but hold it for another half minute."

But he could not.

It went from his hand, and he stood looking at the boy in speechless astonishment.

Wolf gave a growl of satisfaction.

"That's the idea," said Tempest at last, "I've lost five thousand, and my purse too; there's nothing in it though."

"No matter," said the boy, "I only want your purse."

Tempest gave it to him.

"Now," said Wilford, "we will say good night; you see, it is just four minutes and a half."

"Won in a canter," exclaimed his lordship, "what an idiotic muff I shall look like when I go back to Clair; I say, how much will you take for my sword?"

"I will not sell it."

"Oh, that isn't the idea; you don't want a fellow to go home with nothing in his sheath, do you?"

"No."

"But I shall if you don't let me have it back."

"You shall have it."

"That's a good fellow; when?"

"By ten o'clock."

"That's the idea; I shall be at the road-side inn, but of course you will not come there?"

"You are mistaken, my lord, I have promised your friend; I never break my word."

"All right," said Chester, as he sprang into the saddle, "you are a capital fellow, I don't mind losing my wager now."

"Why, my lord."

"Because you are a gentleman," said Chester, giving Wilford his hand; "a fellow who can fight like you do must be a gentleman."

"Thank you," said Wilford gravely, "such an assurance from Lord Tempest Chester gives me great pleasure."

"All right, I daresay; you've done me out of five thousand, you know. But whenever you want a fellow to help you out of a scrape, don't forget Tempest Chester."

So saying he rode away.

"I will not forget," said Wilford to himself, "two such friends may be of service to me on future occasions. By St. George I shall not want assistance in any case if I am fortunate for a little time longer; but let me see, twenty thousand in two days; thirty thousand I have made since I began, that is fifty in all. If the coming year brings me in as much I shall retire; it is a wild life, full of pleasure and excitement too. But it is not—I feel it is not—the life to which I was born; no matter, I am young yet, and have plenty of time to repent and grow virtuous."

While thus soliloquising he had changed his coat, and again looked the richly-dressed graceful youth he had seemed before.

He sheathed his own sword, and concealed the other two beneath his coat. The black plume was taken from his hat and was now in his pocket, together with the mask which had hid his face.

While he was thus engaged, Lord Chester had returned to the inn.

"Hullo!" exclaimed the viscount, "where's your dog?"

"Along with your horse," replied his lordship; "he's got my sword too: and what do you think?"

"I never think," said the viscount.

"For which, perhaps, there is a natural cause," rejoined Chester; "well, don't distress your brains, and I will tell you."

"Do," said Captain Rolfe, "I feel interested."

"Well; the highwayman promised to come here."

"Here!" repeated Captain Rolfe.

"Yes, and he will too; he said so, and he never breaks his word."

"He's going to bring my sword," said the viscount.

"And mine," added Chester, "that's what he's coming for."

"So he told me."

"Then he will not fail," exclaimed Captain Rolfe. "Gentlemen, here is my brother come to claim his wager."

Wilford entered as he spoke.

The clock struck ten.

"By Jove," said the viscount, "Mr. Leander, we have lost the wager."

"Of course," said Wilford, "I knew you would."

"But you didn't know it until I told you."

"Yes I did."

"The deuce!"

"Precisely, he told me so."

"Who did?"

"The gentleman who fought with you," said Wilford quietly.

"What, the Boy Highwayman?"

"Yes."

"By Jove!" said the viscount, "he promised to be here."

"Then he will come," said Wilford, "trust me you will see him soon."

"Shall we! that's the idea," said Captain Rolfe, "give the stakes to the winner, and let us have some more wine."

"Yes," said the viscount, "give him the stakes. By Jove, there goes my five thousand."

"And there goes mine," said Tempest, as Wilford coolly pocketed the money. "Mr. Leander, if the Boy Highwayman was to meet you wouldn't he get a prize."

Wilford laughed.

"He don't seem to come," said Clair; "by Jove, I hope he'll bring my sword."

"So do I," said Chester, "but perhaps he thinks we shall not keep faith with him."

"He never did you so much wrong as to doubt you," exclaimed Wilford.

"Then why the deuce don't he come?"

"He has come."

"Where?"

"Here!" said Wilford, as he threw his coat open, and drew forth the swords. "Now, gentlemen, have I kept my word?"

"The devil!" exclaimed Chester, standing up suddenly, and dropping a glass of wine on the viscount's head, who was sitting staring in stupified amazement at his late antagonist. "That's my sword—the deuce!"

"By Jove!" said Clair, getting up rubbing his head the while; "I say, Tempest, old fellow, what a sell! By Jove!"

Saying which he subsided into a seat.

Captain Rolfe stood looking quietly on.

"But look here!" exclaimed Lord Tempest; "tell us how you did it—I want to know you know. Let me see: you had a black horse, a black dog, a black coat, and a black mask. Ha! I know you did it for a lark—that's the idea! What a capital joke! Don't you see, Clair, he pretended to be the highwayman."

"Of course," said the viscount. "By Jove! Ha, ha!—I see it exactly: he's got my five thousand in his pocket."

"Along with mine," said Lord Tempest. "You did it well; but, I say, how did you get the beautiful Arabian and the big dog?"

"They are both mine," said Wilford, glad to humour their idea that it was a hoax; "you see I do eccentric things sometimes; and when the viscount started the idea of hunting after the Boy Highwayman, I set off intending to personate that individual."

"By Jove, you done it well too—it looked really quite natural."

"It did," said Tempest; "very."

"But the wages was quite fair," said the viscount, "because we need not of known who you were: so you still win."

"I do not wish to keep the stakes," said Wilford: "it was a capital joke, but to retain the stakes would be going too far."

"No," exclaimed Chester; "it's quite fair: we fought, and if you had lost I should have kept your dog."

"So should I," said the viscount; "at least—I mean—the horse."

"Besides," added Chester, "some day we will have a wager, and I'll pretend to be the highwayman: I shall win all the money back then."

"I have a better idea than that," said the viscount.

"Don't say anything about it then," exclaimed his friend; "the last idea you had cost me five thousand."

"Ah; but this is really something worth listening to."

"Let us have it then," said Captain Rolfe.

"So you shall—this is it: what say you, Chester? we will make a party and hunt the Black Wolf."

Wilford started.

"A dangerous expedition," said Captain Rolfe, gravely; "I should advise you not to think of it."

"By Jove! Who cares? I don't. I often used to hunt wolves in France. One wolf hunted me: I should have got the worst of it, too, if I hadn't poked my ramrod through his eye."

"I have heard that tale before," said Chester; "but it's nothing to what I did."

"And what did you do?" asked Wilford.

"Why, it was in France once, you know, near a forest, where the wolves go about in packs and howl: well, I got lost somehow—couldn't find my way anyhow: I tell you, I was in a state—just like the last card in the second suit, in the middle of the pack, you know."

"Go a-head!" said the viscount.

"There was fifty at the least," continued Tempest, "and I had no gun; but I can sing, you know—so I did; I sang something very pathetic, and it had such an effect upon the wolves that they left off howling and began to cry; so I kept on singing till they began to wipe their eyes; and while they were wiping both eyes at once—which of course kept both paws employed at once—I sneaked quietly away. I heard them howl—that was because I didn't stay to sing, you know."

"By Jove!" said the viscount, "what an awful cram!"

"It's true," said Lord Chester; "It does sound odd I know."

"It does indeed," said Wilford with a smile. "To return, however: we were talking of Black Wolf—that, you know, is my mastiff's name, and there he is."

They looked; and Wilford exchanged a look with Captain Rolfe, as he saw that the mastiff kept his nose close down to the trap-door.

He growled fiercely, and turned to his master as though to ask his aid: finally, he seized the iron ring in his strong teeth, and pulled the trap open.

"There's somebody there," said Wilford, "Mr. Landlord, what do you keep in your cellar?"

"Nothing particular," said Long Jack, coming forward hurriedly, "he smells a rat perhaps."

"I think he does," said Wilford, significantly; "gentlemen, let's hunt for the rat in the cellar."

"That's the idea," shouted Chester, "I've got some bait."

He flourished his sword, and made several ferocious thrusts at some imaginary adversary.

At that moment Bessie's face appeared at the side window of the little room.

Wilford saw her, though the rest did not.

The viscount and his friend were at the trap door, while Long Jack was expostulating loudly against their attempts to descend.

Wolf growled and looked fiercely, and there was a general row.

So the boy took advantage of the moment, and stole to Bessie's side.

"You are as white as a little ghost," he whispered, putting his arm around her waist, and pressing her for an instant to his breast.

"What is the matter?"

"There are three men down there," she answered rapidly, even in her wish to save him, thinking of her father; "it is not father's fault, they would go."

"He shall not be hurt," said Wilford; "but now go to your room."

He kissed her cold lips, and returned to the trap door.

Under any other circumstances his first impulse would have been to run his sword through the treacherous landlord's body; as it was, however, he compromised the matter by thinking of pretty Bessie's love for himself.

But he sternly ordered Long Jack away, and prepared to descend.

"Come, gentlemen," he said, "the rats are in the trap; let's catch them."

Lord Tempest gave a shout, and, securing a light, lowered himself down by the edge of the trap, and dropped into the cellar.

Long Jack's face went like ashes.

"It will be their own fault if they go too far," he thought, "because they won't find their way out."

But in this speculation he was taken in.

Lord Chester, the Viscount, and Wilford descended; but Captain Rolfe did not.

He had some suspicion of his worthy host, and thought it would be well to keep an eye on him.

Which he did.

The mastiff had been the first to leap down, and, having so done, he sat down and growled with astonishment.

The gentlemen stared.

Save for themselves, there was nobody in the cellar.

"That's odd!" exclaimed his lordship, "what sort of rats were they, Mr. Leander?"

"Such as they breed in Bow Street," replied the youth; "they are very skilful in hiding away."

"I wonder what they wanted."

"I think it was the Boy Highwayman."

"That was you."

"Precisely."

"The audacious rascals. What! that would have spoiled the joke."

"By Jove, yes," said the President; "so it would."

Wilford thought so too.

"Your dog seems at fault," observed his lordship; "he's smelling at a cask of ale."

"Take the bung out, and look through the hole," suggested Clair.

Lord Tempest was innocent enough to do so.

He inserted the point of his sword in the bung, and dexterously jerked it out.

The President was standing in front of the cask as his friend acted on his suggestion, and, directly the bung was out, a swift stream of strong ale shot straight out of the hole, and Clair was smothered in no time.

The first shock sent him on his back, and the cask was half empty before he could get out of the way.

"By Jove," he said, springing to his feet, completely drenched and covered with sawdust; "why didn't you wait till I moved."

"Never mind, old boy," said Chester; "you will soon get dry."

"Yes—but see how I shall smell; people will take me for a brewer."

If his lordship had not been so prompt to act he would have seen that Wolf left the cask, after a mere cursory inspection, and went to another, on the outside of which he scratched.

Wilford tapped it with the hilt of his sword.

"Is anybody at home?" asked Lord Chester.

"I think there is," said Wilford, as he took the bung out, "anyhow it is not more than two feet deep with liquor."

This he had ascertained by tapping it, until he found that the lower he went the less hollow was the sound.

He now put his sword through the bung-hole.

"That's the idea," said his lordship, "dig away."

Wilford did, and his first dig extorted a yell from Tiger Blue.

The point of the sword had gone through his coat-tail, and pinned it to a prominent part of his body.

"Bravo!" shouted Chester, "let him have it."

"By Jove!" cried the viscount, "bring them out and roll them in the wet."

"Not if I know it," exclaimed a voice, and Hunter's head appeared above the top of the cask, "stand back, or somebody will get a bullet."

He presented a brace of pistols as he spoke.

"By Jove," said the viscount, as he hit him in the face with a large handful of wet sawdust, "take your ugly head out of sight."

The ugly head disappeared, and the owner went down with a splash.

Then Wilford and his two companions turned the cask on its side, and rolled it over and over.

There was not much in it, still there was enough to make the officers and Tiger Blue miserably wet; and as quickly as they could they scrambled out, ran up the ladder and out of the house.

They each got a smart bite from Wolf, and a kick from his master and his master's companions.

"That's the idea," said Chester, "I think they have had enough."

They had, for the present, at least, though they did not give up their intention of capturing the daring boy.

They lurked near the house, waiting till Wilford's companions should depart, which two of them did soon after, the two being the viscount—still very wet—and Lord Tempest Chester, in high glee at the result of their ratcatching.

Captain Rolfe now remained with his brother for awhile.

"Where do you go to-night?" asked the Captain.

"To Wayncliffe Grange," replied the youth, "will you accompany me."

"Great heavens, no! Wayncliffe Grange, not there for worlds."

Wilford looked at him in strange surprise.

Captain Rolfe was ghastly pale, and trembled from head to foot.

--------

## CHAPTER VII.

### THE MAN WITH THE MARK UPON HIS BROW.

CAPTAIN ROLFE was not what he seemed.

Wilford had thought so before; but never had the thought presented itself with such force as now.

A mystery hung over the captain's past life, and those that knew him best knew but little.

It was strange that the mention of Wayncliffe Grange should so strongly affect him.

In general he was singularly calm, rarely moved to mirth or anger, somewhat stern, always grave but kind, and with an habitual cast of thought upon his

WILFORD AND ALICE AT THE GRANGE

brow, which told that he had the memory of some sadness in his heart.

Wilford looked at him and wondered much.

Why should his face turn suddenly so white, and his dark eye look with such remorseful agony upon his young companion.

He had been kind and affectionate to him always; brave, patient, devoted, and unselfish.

Wilford could have staked his soul that Captain Rolfe had never wronged a living creature.

But it was very strange to see him thus.

"What is the matter Rolfe?"

Wilford took the other's strong hand which trembled like an aspen leaf.

"Nothing, Wilford, nothing; do not ask me now?"

"But you are agitated; your cheek is pale and your looks are wild; surely there is something strange in this."

No. 4.

"No matter, do not question me; but tell me what you do at the Grange."

He spake the last word with a shudder.

Still wondering, Wilford related the adventure in which he had saved the fair Alice from the two masked horsemen.

Captain Rolfe listened with intense interest.

"There is destiny in this," he muttered, when the boy had finished; "the strong just power that shapes everything as it may think best, and all for its own good purpose. Strange that they should meet there —strange—very strange."

His head dropped upon his breast, and he became lost in meditation.

"Of what are you thinking?" asked Wilford, at length. "Come, Rolfe, this is no time for reveries; tell me why you seemed so surprised."

"Would that I dared."

"Dared! what should prevent you?"

"An oath—a dark fearful oath, which sits like a weight of iron on my soul—an oath from which I can only be set free by the death of him to whom I swore it."

"And he?"

"To one whose name I dare not breathe. It must be told some day, and then, Wilford, then—"

"What then?"

"You will hate me—curse me as the evil spirit who has blighted your destiny—think upon me with dark and bitter scorn, and bitterness which I have deserved but too well."

"Never, Rolfe, never!" cried the boy passionately; "hate you, my friend—the kindest and most generous heart I ever knew; never, Rolfe, my brother!"

"Brother?"

"Why do you repeat the word in a tone so strange; you are my brother, are you not?"

"Do you doubt it, Wilford?" exclaimed the other, in a tone which showed how deeply he was moved by the question; "did I ever give you cause to think me otherwise?"

"No, Rolfe, no; forgive me. I have pained you deeply, I can see. I do not doubt you; you have ever been most kind to me; but your words were so strange—you were so agitated when I spoke of Lord Wayncliffe."

"Not that name, for heaven's sake; as you love me, do not breathe that name to me again."

Wilford put his arm around the captain's neck.

He loved his brother with a strong deep love, and could not bear to see him moved, as now he was.

The boy recalled a time when he had been stricken down by a bullet, within a month after he first took to the road, and he recollected well how Captain Rolfe had fought like a lion to defend him.

Then when their many foes were beaten back, and Rolfe had carried him to their home, he thought of how, night after night, his brave champion had sat by his couch, and nursed him back to life, with a tenderness and care almost womanly.

So thinking more of the handsome anxious face that had bent above his pillow, of the kind strong hand whose touch had been so gentle, and the dark eyes that had never wearied, though they grew haggard and worn with watching, Wilford kept his arm around the other's neck, as he said—

"Come, Rolfe; forget that I ever spoke it, and will not do so again; more, if it pains you, I will not go there."

"God forbid that I should stand between you," said the captain earnestly. "Go there, Wilford, and learn to cherish well the man whose child you saved."

"Do you know him?"

"Do I not? ask me no more, but depart at once; see, it is very late; they will wonder at your absence. Good night, Wilford."

He took the boy in his arms, and kissed his white expansive brow, then wrung his hand, and went to the door.

Before the youth could follow, Captain Rolfe was in the saddle and riding up the road towards London.

He left Wilford in a state of conjecture.

The more he thought of it, the more strange it seemed.

Then, in some inexpressible manner, he began to associate Captain Rolfe with the story told by Lord Wayncliffe.

But each self-suggestion only made the matter more incomprehensive; so the boy finally resolved to think no more.

It was one of those dark mysteries from which the veil can only be torn by the hand of time.

There is something more than strange in the way that a crime, once committed, increases link by link, until it forms a long chain of guilt and mystery, which in the end is sure to wind around the perpetrator, until its numberless evils crush him down to dishonour and destruction.

On whose head rested the guilt of that crime which had destroyed the happiness of Lord Wayncliffe's life, remains yet to be seen. It was a cruel deed, and very strange was the story of its doing.

But it had a startling and a bloody sequel.

We may not tell it yet, but, when told, it will form a history more wild and marvellous than ever yet was given to the world.

The bold fearless boy, whose daring deeds will be chronicled in this strange story, was, although he knew it not, the instrument chosen by destiny to bring peace and gladness to the innocent and wronged—mercy to those who, though erring, were repentant—and deep and dire retribution to the blood-stained man of crime.

Let us follow him as, step by step, he travels through his wayward career.

He was going now to Wayncliffe Grange.

Before he went he called the landlord.

"Who were those men you had concealed in the cellar?" he asked sternly.

Long Jack had a lie ready made.

"They was only some poor devils as had the grabs after 'em."

"Indeed," said Wilford, doubtfully. "Well, be advised, my friend, and take care who you shelter in your cellar for the future."

"All right, captain; you don't think as they was anybody as wanted you, do you?"

"Yes, I do; don't you?"

"No, captain—'cos if I had, I'd have learned 'em different."

"Doubtless; but keep true to the band, as even my regard for Bessie will not save you."

So saying, he took leave of Bessie and the house.

"Your regard, as you calls it, won't save you, if ever I get a chance to do you a turn," muttered Long Jack; "you're mighty high, and don't care which way your coin goes; but I've got enough of my own, and Jack Long ain't to be bought or frightened out of his revenge."

And mine host of the "Shepherd" closed his house and went to bed, brooding over schemes of vengeance, and trying to drown other unpleasant recollections in deep draughts of raw brandy.

He did not rest long.

Tiger Blue and the officers had followed Wilford stealthily till he passed through the lodge gate, on his way to the Grange, and, having seen him so far, they returned to the inn.

"So he's there, is he," muttered Tiger; "I'll have him now; he couldn't a gone to a better place for me."

The ruffian saw a better chance now of obtaining not only the reward, but some additional revenge for one or two things he could not forget: one was the red cross on his hand, the other was the hole made by the point of Wilford's sword in the most uncomfortable part of Tiger Blue's animal economy.

There was one person in the Grange with whom the ruffian was well acquainted.

They had done some work together many years ago.

They were familiar sometimes now, only it was when they were in some place remote from the gaze of curious people, who might, perhaps, have wondered what a gentleman could have to say to such a brutal-looking wretch as Tiger Blue.

When Wilford reached the Grange, he saw two gentlemen present whom he had not seen before.

At least, he did not recognise them.

The elder of the two was introduced as Sir Richard Wayncliffe.

He was Lord Wayncliffe's only brother.

He had a face which might have been thought handsome, but for a peculiar look in the keen dark eye, narrow, and set deep behind the scowling brow; but he was polished, well bred, and unmistakably a Wayncliffe.

He welcomed Wilford cordially, and praised his

skill and courage highly, and thanked him warmly for having rescued his brother's ward.

"You will be friends, I know," exclaimed his lordship. "Mr. Leander is already deep in my regard, and you, Richard, will, I hope, learn to like him as well."

"If I may speak from the impression made by this our first meeting," said the baronet, courteously, "my regard, Mr. Leander, is not less than yours."

This was very flattering, and Wilford made a graceful answer; but he did not like Sir Richard, though he had no reason for his antipathy.

Then the other one was introduced.

He was young, rather prepossessing, but with an expression of indecision and want of character in his face, which somewhat marred the effect his good looks might have otherwise created.

He was just such a man as might have been made into something very noble or very base: he was easily led, fond of pleasure, slightly vicious, and occasionally vulgar.

These last were the fault of bad example, and passions, which, through the want of careful training, had degenerated into coarseness.

His name was Lord Edward Horton.

Such were the two in whose company Wilford found himself, and, from some cause or other, he watched them very closely.

The hour was late, so Alice had retired to her chamber, not, however, without some regret that she did not see her young preserver ere she went. She would have stayed had it not been for Lord Horton's presence, but his coarse attentions only sickened her, and she retired to think with more pleasure of the handsome youth, who seemed more so when placed in silent comparison with her titled admirer.

So, the fair lady not being present, Wilford devoted himself more attentive to his host. Sir Richard, and Sir Richard's friend.

To the last two more especially.

And to Sir Richard in particular.

They conversed for a long time on many things, in all of which the boy shone to advantage.

Horton, who was well up in all things concerning fast or fashionable life, was soon left nowhere.

Wilford's words were all well chosen—brilliant, terse, and to the point.

Then his style was so graceful; even if he only raised his hand, or turned his head, every attitude, every look was easy, elegant, and natural.

Yet he was quiet, never obtrusive, always listened attentively, and did not speak save when his words were well timed.

Sir Richard was a man of good conversation: in fact it was to his tongue that he owed his rank in life and success at court, but the polished classic style of language which came so easily from Wilford's lips possessed a much greater charm than the studied phrases of the courtier.

As for Lord Edward, he very wisely subsided down to "yes" and "no," which he said alternately as occasion served, and sometimes said the wrong word, in doing which he would empty a large glass of wine and swear mentally, at a rate awful to contemplate.

Somehow or other he said the wrong word so many times, and consoled himself by emptying the glass on every occasion, that at last he began to think it was all right, said he knew all about it, tol-de-rol, and didn't care a straw for old Dick Wayn—hic—cliff, and wound up by declaring that he would fight the best swordsmen that ever rode a black Arabian mastiff, if he'd only tell the horse not to bite.

After which he fell out of his chair and rolled underneath the table, where he lay muttering incoherent defiance at everybody, including old Dick, who had won an awful lot of money, which he would see him damned before he'd pay, unless he had the lovely Alice before he went away.

He said such envious things that Sir Richard began to feel uncomfortable, but an observation from Wilford set him again at ease.

"Your friend wonders in his cups," he said, as though pitying the helpless drunkard, "he seems to have associated the story of my adventure with his own feelings in some peculiar manner; it is strange how soon the influence of drink will scatter a man's senses, and make his intellect powerless."

"It is also sad that it should be so," said Lord Wayncliffe, "but the custom of the age make such occurrences as these too common and general for observation."

He rang the bell, and a couple of servants entered.

"Let Lord Horton be taken to his room."

But Lord Horton didn't see it.

He swore that the first man who touched him should have his eye bunged up; and the ancestral founders of our present row of pampered menials had too much respect for their optics to trust themselves within reach of his lordship's heavy hand.

He now sat upright, supporting himself in that position by holding on to his foot; and then began to give vent to his long suppressed eloquence in a style for which his extreme drunkenness could be his only excuse.

"I know," he began, "you want to get me out of the way; but I won't go—hic. Old Dick's afraid I shall let out too much; but you'd better not come within reach of my clutch. I think I have had—hic—a little too much, you had better keep back, as you may get a touch on your nose, which may—hic—spoil its shape: so look out, for I know very well—hic—what I am about," in proof of which he got up and staggered from the room, steadying himself by hanging on to the servants by the hair, and in that interesting position he was carried to his apartment, where he howled out defiance at disjointed intervals till the morning, when he sank into a heavy sleep, and woke up with some sense of dread at the idea that he may have given utterance to words which had better have been left unsaid.

He had got the grace to feel heartily ashamed of himself, but that did not efface the recollection of the scene from Lord Wayncliff's mind.

Wilford watched him leave the room with a look of deep disgust.

He saw that Sir Richard seemed embarrassed by his friend's inebriated mutterings, and having some suspicions that they were not without foundation, said abruptly—

"Do you think, my Lord, that we shall ever discover the identity of the two ruffians who waylaid your niece?"

Sir Richard started visibly as the peer replied.

"It is more than probable; he bears a mark by which it would be easy to recognise him!"

Wilford kept his eye keenly fixed on the baronet's face.

"Have you any clue which might give you an idea as to the motive?" he asked.

"None," replied Lord Wayncliffe.

Just then the mastiff, who had missed his master, began scratching at the door.

"It is your dog, Mr. Leander," observed his lordship, "let him come in, poor fellow, he is really a magnificent animal."

Wilford opened the door.

Wolf came into the room; but no sooner did he see Sir Richard than he displayed his teeth and gave a deep savage growl.

"Down, Wolf," said Wilford, seeing that the baronet's face turned pale, "really, Sir Richard, I must apologize for his bad behaviour."

A small bronze statuette stood on a slender column of black marble close by the baronet's chair, and as he turned to answer Wilford, his arm struck against the pedestal, and the bronze figure fell.

It just grazed Sir Richard's forehead, scarcely striking him with sufficient force to have hurt a child; yet, when he put his handkerchief to the spot, it became saturated with blood in a moment.

"Art you hurt, Richard?" asked the peer anxiously,

"It is nothing, a mere scratch, I fell from my horse while riding here, and received a slight cut from a sharp stone."

"Thank heaven it's no worse," said his brother, "being on your brow it might have been very dangerous."

"It might, indeed," exclaimed Wilford, with a peculiar intonation of voice, "such wounds always leave a scar, that only the grave can hide."

Nothing more was said; but Wilford saw that both his lordship and Sir Richard attached some strangely ominous significance to the incident.

He was not acquainted with the history of the Wayncliffe family, or he would have known that there was a singular legend in connection with that little bronze figure of the warrior, who stood sword in hand on the black marble pedestal. But Wilford now *knew the man who bore the mark upon his brow.*

---

## CHAPTER VIII.

### A TALE OF TREACHERY AND DREAMS OF LOVE.

LORD WAYNCLIFFE never once suspected that the serpent who had stung him to the soul was his brother—the man he loved most of all on earth.

Yet so it was.

The poisoned venom of the snake is never more dangerous and deadly than when it is veiled like a thing of beauty by the fireside.

It was a devilish plot!

More like some fabled story of a hideous invention than a tale of life.

Looking at that grave polished gentleman, you would not have thought that he could coolly sit and brood over the means most certain to destroy his brother's peace.

Yet he had done so.

He was a cruel crafty man—this baronet—Sir Richard Wayncliffe.

Seeming just and honourable to his fellow man,—envied for his rank, and proud for his influence,—he was a man in whose path it was dangerous to stand.

He was a gambler and a libertine.

In his younger days he had loved, with such love as he could feel, a young and beautiful lady, whose wealth would have cleared the heavy debts and difficulties in which he was involved.

He would have wooed and won her, but for one unexpected abstract which suddenly arose.

His brother married her instead.

The simple fact, that he should wed at all was exceedingly objectionable to Richard—he was not a baronet then; but still more objectionable that he should wed the lady of Richard's choice.

Lord Wayncliffe was totally unconscious of having crossed his brother's love, and Richard did not tell him he had done so.

On the contrary: he congratulated him on his happiness, and always was most respectful and affectionate to the lady.

It is not often that a younger brother displays so much disinterested pleasure, as did Richard Wayncliffe, on the occasion of his brother's wedding.

His joy was greater still when, a year later, Lady Wayncliffe gave birth to a son and heir.

His lordship could not help thinking, at times, what a noble and generous fellow he had got for a brother.

So kind to Lady Wayncliffe, too.

It was very strange; but her ladyship had never looked upon him with any great degree of partiality.

Not all his soft voice or persuasive grace could win her favour.

She seemed instinctively to know his nature.

And a base, wicked nature it was.

He was ambitious and revengeful.

Not only had his brother deprived him of his love, but now he had deprived him of the hope he had cherished of one day having the inheritance.

True, they were yet to be obtained.

*But how?*

It was a question which could scarcely find an answer—even in the black soul of the questioner.

Two lives stood in the way.

His brother's wife and child.

It was strange that he could think of doing harm to those who were so beautiful and innocent.

Yet he could coolly and deliberately lay a snare for the honour of the one, and the life of the other.

Let it be understood that we are now giving in detail the story told by Lord Wayncliffe to Wilford.

It will be seen by this how complicated was the mystery.

Richard Wayncliffe was not long ere he thought of means.

His brother was absent on a trial in London.

Save for the servants, the sole occupants of the Grange were Lady Wayncliffe, her child, her husband's brother, and a gentleman guest, by name Lord Henry Rivers.

Lord Rivers was a young nobleman whom Richard Wayncliffe had, by the power of his evil influence, led into the reckless pleasures of his own dishonourable life.

The unfortunate youth became enthralled by the cursed infatuation of the gaming-table, until, little by little, his princely wealth was gone, and he was left upon the world penniless and a beggar.

The dark tempter was ever at his side, urging him to desperate means, and, in an evil hour, he was persuaded to raise a heavy sum of money by means of a forged signature, purporting to be his father's.

Let it not be thought that he yielded easily to this.

The tempting devil who had brought him to ruin lured him on by false hopes, and the young man thought that in the wealth thus gained he had the means of retrieving his past losses.

But he lost that money as he had the rest; and the time came when the forged bill must be paid, or he be branded as a felon, and consigned to a disgraceful doom.

The punishment of forgery was death on the scaffold.

If his crime once became known, he would be hanged.

So, in the time of his danger and despair, he appealed to his friend—his friend, the demon, who had led him to dishonour—Richard Wayncliff.

And in his time of need Richard did not desert him.

He paid the money, but retained possession of the fatal document.

And in that he held a rod of iron which made the young nobleman his slave.

So much so, that when Richard Wayncliff proposed his diabolical plot, Lord Rivers dared not resist the strong power which forced him to share the infamy.

The plan was thus arranged:—

Lord Rivers was to take the child, either to kill or go to some land, but never return to England under pain of being delivered up to justice as a forger.

He was also bound by a fearful oath never to reveal, at any time or place, his share in the transaction while Richard Wayncliff lived.

He felt that he could, without remorse, have strangled the bloodless villain who made him do a task so revolting.

That this, stronger than all his rage, was the knowledge of that fearful secret by which the other could at any moment send him to an awful death.

So, thinking that the time might yet come when he would be able to do justice unto those he was thus forced to wrong, he took the child, and in the dead of night stole away.

And that same night, when the inhabitants of the

Grange were locked in slumber, Richard Wayncliff went like a second Tarquin to the chamber of his brother's wife, and, like a ruthless devil, mocking all her tearful prayers and bitter agony, took her from that sacred couch in which so oft she had laid by her husband's side, and bore her thence unto a place where he knew she would be kept from human gaze.

He would have forced her to become a victim to his brutal passions, but her hate for him was stronger than her love for life, and he saw that she would rather die than yield.

So he placed her in the care of those whom he knew would be deaf to all her prayers, and having thus completed his infernal work, he returned to the Grange.

He had set a spy on to watch Lord Rivers, and in that he did not break his promise, giving him instructions to slay both him and the child if he saw a chance.

The spy came back to say that it was done.

He had, he said, tracked them to a lonely inn, and murdered them in bed.

Richard Wayncliff would have had his brother's wife murdered too, but villain though he was, his soul recoiled from the thought of shedding her blood.

But it was not merciful to let her live.

The fate to which he gave her was worse than death.

He took her to a private madhouse.

A place kept by a monster who was well used to such cases.

He could have told some startling secrets, but it paid him better to keep them unknown.

There were many in that prison-house who had gone there in the full possession of their faculties.

They did not keep them long.

Such deeds were done there as would have caused even the executioner of the Ancient Inquisition to shudder.

Once committed to the keeper's care it was not long before the victim was a raving maniac.

So having thus put her out of the way, Richard Wayncliffe gave out that she had eloped with Lord Henry Rivers.

His own grief for his brother's affliction was so well assumed that no one suspected him.

Such a thought was never once entertained for a moment by Lord Wayncliffe.

He lived on, a saddened stricken man, never even in all the long weary years that passed losing faith in his wife's honour, or forgetting the love with which he loved her.

Fourteen years passed away, and still Sir Richard lived his life of sin.

He had won the rank of baronet; been presented with a place in parliament; gained immense wealth in some mysterious manner; yet he was not rich.

A curse seemed to hang over him; the infatuation of gaming still clung to him, and whatever wealth he won he was sure to lose again.

As a last resource he had introduced Lord Horton to Alice with an understanding that if she married him the successful wooer was to give Sir Richard half his fortune.

But Alice had rejected him at once, and it was then they pursued the plan of her abduction from which she had been saved by Wilford's gallant interposition.

The rest of this history we have seen.

It was the morning after Wilford's return to the Grange.

Sir Richard was with Lord Horton, discussing plans which bodied no good, either to Alice or her young preserver. Lord Wayncliffe was in the library busied with his law books, so Wilford improved the opportunity and went for a ride with Alice.

Sir Richard and his companion watched them with a dark scowl as the handsome youth assisted Alice to the saddle.

Then, mounting Selim's back, he set off in company with the fair girl, followed, as usual, by the mastiff.

A bright flush was on her cheek, and her eyes were full of light—soft liquid light, which told of sweet thoughts and dreams of happiness.

And Wilford, handsome and graceful as he was at all times, had never looked to such advantage as he did now.

His slender form and dark face were as beautiful as any ever sculptured by the chisel of an artist, and so thought the lady as he rode beside her with his long black hair sweeping back from his white brow, or, as he inclined his head, falling over his cheek and veiling the brilliance of his large flashing eyes.

It was to her a face without a fault, perfect in feature and noble in expression, the profile was classic and singularly bold, somewhat too bold at times; for bright and beautiful as now it looked, there were times when it was so stern and pitiless that strong men would tremble for their lives.

But now it was very calm and gentle, and the proud dark eyes were subdued as though he too was dreaming dreams of happiness.

He was thinking of the lady by his side, and in truth she was one who might well set the soul bewitching with such thoughts as are most natural to youth.

He looked upon her fair face shaded by its wreath of sunny tresses, then upon her deep blue eyes, so earnest and dream-like as they were, then his gaze wandered to her white neck, rising graceful as the throat of a swan from her high swelling bust, thence to her waist, encircled by a sash as small as that which may have bound Diana's robe, then he suffered his glance to rest for a moment on her exquisite limbs, whose sweeping length and swelling curves could be distinctly traced through the folds of her riding-dress.

And looking at her thus, he thought how beautiful she was, and thinking so, he sighed.

It was strange, perhaps, that he should do so; but the recollection of his way of life made him sad, when he thought that, although he might win her love, he could not in honour ask her to be his bride.

They rode on in silence for some time, when Alice said—

"Your horse is a beautiful creature, Mr Leander."

The boy looked at the noble Arabian, and, patting his glossy neck, said—

"He has no equal; I would not lose him for a king's ransom."

"You seem greatly attached to him?"

"We love each other very much; it is a strange term to use, perhaps, but it is true, and he deserves it well, for he has saved my life on more than one occasion; in truth, if it were not for the noble fellow, and his friend the mastiff, I should not now have the pleasure of riding by your side,"

"You have been in danger then?" said Alice, looking with much interest at her young companion.

The boy laughed.

"Occasionally I am somewhat reckless, you know, and only live in wild excitement; in fact I have had a grave idea of taking to the road."

He spoke as though testingly, but watched closely to see what effect the words would have on Alice.

He saw her cheek turn pale, and his heart pained him.

"Heaven forbid;" she exclaimed fervently, "it must be a fearful life to live."

"Do you think so?" he said, gravely: "nay, then, I will tell you a secret."

"A secret?"

"Yes; but I must not now."

"Oh, why?"

"Come," he said, as they turned into a shady avenue, "let us sit beneath that stately oak there, and I will tell you a story strange and true."

Alice laughed gaily.

"What story will you tell?" she asked, "will it be some ancient legend, full of mystery and wild adventure?"

"Something of both," replied Wilford, as he sprang from his saddle, and assisted his companion to alight, "of mystery and adventure too, but the burden is an old one."

His heart leaped as her hand rested on his shoulder, and the quick blood mounted to his cheek, as in raising her skirt to descend he caught a momentary glimpse of a tiny little foot, and something more than the turn of a most beautiful little ankle he had ever seen.

"What a lovely limb," he murmured unconsciously.

Alice did not catch the observation.

"What did you say?" she asked innocently.

"That you are a superb equestrian," he answered, recollecting himself, and leading her to a seat, he fastened the horses' reins to a bough, then returned and threw himself on the ground by her side.

Wolf wagged his tail and looked sagaciously at his master, and then like a well bred dog as he was, turned his head away and looked at Selim.

Selim looked at him, and both seemed as though they knew all about it.

Alice sat on a low Gothic seat, and Wilford reclined on the sward by her side.

"Come here?" he said to Wolf, who came forward at a bound, and laid down just behind his master, who threw an arm carelessly over his favourite's broad back, and disposing his graceful body in an attitude at once elegant and easy, the boy raised his face towards his fair companion, and said—

"Lady, shall I be your page?"

"My page!" said Alice, blushing as her eyes met his, "that is a strange request."

"But will you grant it?"

"I see no reason to repence; but why choose such a character? why not for the time be a cavelier, a wandering minstrel, or some brave knight errant, such as we read of in some sporting romance."

"Because," said Wilford, as he took her little hand, "a page may love his mistress only, while those minstrels, cavaliers, and knight errants that you read of, were remarkable for their inconstancy, as for their gallantry and devotion. Now, a page is always faithful, and cares alone for the sweet lady he may serve; so let me be your page, that I may love you?"

"Then you must be obedient as well, or as a mistress I may prove unkind."

"I don't care; you will not banish me I know."

"Perhaps. Ladies, you know, are wayward: but may I ask Mr. Leander—"

"Wilford; I am your page, you know."

"Wilford then!" exclaimed Alice, dwelling with a thrill of pleasure on the name; "may I ask Wilford, if it is a page's privilege to keep the hand of his mistress so closely in his own?"

"Unquestionably, I never read anything to the contrary, sometimes their priviledge was greater still."

"But not until they had been longer in the lady's service."

Wilford pressed his lips to the little hand he held.

"Love is not told by time," he said earnestly, "a life's period may sometimes pass in one swift hour of joy."

"Is it part of a page's office to teach his mistress how to love?"

"His first and dearest. Can I think you teach the lady Alice to love me?"

"I cannot tell you yet."

The boy's heart throbbed with joy as he heard how low and tremulous her voice had grown.

"Let me tell my story, then," he said, rising to his knee, "but first tell me what shall be my reward?"

Little by little as he spoke his arm glided round her slender waist, and he could feel her heart beating rapidly as he drew her gently towards him.

She did not struggle or try to disengage herself; her eyes swam, and her cheeks glowed with a deeper and more vivid crimson; but her love was stronger than her bashfulness, and when he pressed her to his breast she did not by word or look resist.

He held her there for some time, and neither spoke; but their flushed cheeks and burning eyes gave utterance to a silent language more eloquent than words—it was one of the moments when the heart seems to stand still, and the blood scarcely stirs in the veins, while every nerve is held enthralled in Love's wondrous spell.

Such moments in life are few and far between—they can only be known when the heart is young, and every sense is full of vivid life—they are moments beautiful to know and sweet to recollect, for not all the toil and bitterness of dreary years thrown afterwards, when youth is passed and the charm of beauty is for ever lost, can deprive the heart of the strong memory of such moments, known when the heart was passionate and pure.

It was such a time now with our hero and the lovely Alice, and she had remained in his arms for many minutes ere she said, while partly withdrawing from his embrace—

"You have not earned your reward yet, Wilford; tell me the story."

"But will you not pay me in anticipation?"

He looked into her eyes, and there read an answering expression.

Then tenderly and gently he drew her head downwards, and their lips clung together in a long silent kiss.

"You know the story now," he said, as they sat side by side, "do you not?"

"Is it that you love me?"

"Sweet sibyl, yes."

"And was this your secret?"

"It was, darling; why do you ask?"

"Because it was mine too," she answered as he caught her again in his arms, and covered her lovely face with passionate caresses.

"Alice," he asked suddenly, "why do you love me?"

It seemed so very strange a question to ask at such a time, that it is no wonder the maiden looked at him in surprise.

"Come," he continued, kneeling at her feet and clasping both hands round her waist as she sat, "I will tell you."

Her soft snowy head was resting caressingly on dark hair clustering over his brow, and her innocent confiding eyes looked inquiringly into his.

Perhaps she thought he had set himself a somewhat difficult task.

His dark boyish face was very grave, despite the smile of love with which every lineament was lit, and he gazed upon her with a look which seemed to search her very soul.

"You love me," he said, at last, "because the circumstances under which we met were such as might cause your heart to beat with gentle thoughts for me—you felt some gratitude, perchance, and admired a daring act, which, although done in your sweet service, was as nothing to what I sometimes have to do for myself."

She listened to him, silent, still, and wondering much.

"I seem to you a young gentleman of fortune—youthful, rich, somewhat accomplished, and with such attributes of face and form as a lady loves to see."

"I have such attributes, I know, and in saying so I am not egotistical, for to deny that we have such gifts is to be ungrateful unto heaven, and to nature, and if I had them not I know you would not care for me. Well, then, seeming thus, I love you, and win your affection in return. Is it not so?"

"You are brave and beautiful, honourable and true, it is for that I love you—not for your wealth, nor yet for your position."

"But what if I were not what I seem? what if I were one about whose way of life there is a mystery—whose fortune has been gained by desperate means: suppose I were to tell you that my career is one of danger and dishonour, and that a price was set upon my head?"

"I should not believe you, Wilford. Dear Wilford, how strangely you speak! Why do you say such things?"

"Tell me, Alice, what if they were true?"

"But they are not—I cannot think it, Wilford: do not jest with such an earnest brow."

The boy looked sadly at her.

"Answer me as though it were no jest. Could you love me in dishonour? if my brow was scored with shame, and my soul stained with crime, tell me, would you cherish me with thoughts of tenderness? or would the knowledge strike your heart and make you turn from me in sorrow?"

"Never, Wilford! never!" said Alice, passionately, "I could not love you less. I would cling to you through all, even though my heart would break to think that you were in danger, or that you were not what I have dreamed you were."

"Then heaven keep you from such knowledge," exclaimed Wilford, "but let me ask you never to doubt my love, whatever you may see or hear: there is a mystery attached to my career which I may not yet unfold; but though the mystery is strange, it does not veil a life of crime."

"Then I do not wish to know it," exclaimed Alice, from whose heart the boy's last words had raised a load of apprehension, "I care not for the rest, so that your soul is free from crime."

"It is, I swear to heaven!" said her lover, as again he pressed his lips to hers; then, rising from his knees, he released the horses reins from the bough, and assisted her to the saddle.

It is a task singularly graceful and agreeable, that of aiding a lady to mount her steed.

It is a sacred office, only suited to a lover, for who but a lover should have the lady's hand on his shoulder, and her little foot within his hand? The very attitude breathes of love and confidence: though to the innocent mind of Alice, there was nothing in the act to cause her lover's cheek to glow and his hand to tremble: but to him there was something very strange and thrilling in the momentary touch of her bust against his shoulder, and though as he adjusted her foot in the stirrup he only caught a passing glimpse of her lovely ancle in its white silken covering, it was enough to make the glow deepen on his cheek, and set his heart dreaming strange dreams.

The sterner sex are the weakest after all. If old Diogenes had been called from his tub to assist a lady to mount her horse or descend from the saddle, we believe he would have growled more savagely than ever, and found, despite his growling, his cynical philosophy strangely mixed up somehow with thoughts of glistening eyes, fair faces, tiny feet, white necks, little hands, and pretty ancles.

Such things must possess some peculiar magnetism of their own—they are dangerous to see and still more dangerous to touch. Why it should be so we know not, unless it is that Byron speaks the truth when he says—

"Man's a strange animal, and makes strange use
Of his own nature."

Or again, when he tells us that—

"Man's a phenomenon, one knows not what,
And wonderful beyond all wondrous measure.
'Tis pity, though, in this sublime world that
Pleasure's a sin, and sometimes sin's a pleasure.
Few mortals know what end they would be at—
But whether glory, or power, or love, or treason,
The path is through perplexing ways, and when
The goal is gained we die, you know, and then——"

With which extremely lucid conclusion we coincide most fully, as did our hero, Wilford Leander.

He was by nature strongly passionate, and saw no sin in loving as he loved. His thoughts were pure, for her loveliness was just of that sort that makes a sense of adoration rather than desire. She was very trusting, almost too much so, perhaps: but Wilford was never one to wrong a maiden's faith, unless they were thrown together in such a situation as made it impossible to resist, because there are times when there is no resistance.

It had been so with pretty Bessie, who had loved Wilford purely for his personal grace and beauty; but with Alice it was different, she was highborn and proud, and her mind, naturally pure, had been kept so by careful education, she was free therefore from such impulses as had tempted Bessie to her fall; the one was a lady whose birth and position kept her sacred from such unholy words or thoughts; the other was a simple untaught child of nature, who had no position to lose, and saw no sin in yielding gladly to the passionate libertinism of the youth she loved.

Poor Bessie! Wilford was thinking of her now with some regret, and mentally comparing her with the maiden by his side, in which he was perhaps ungenerous, for her thoughts were solely occupied by him.

They were riding slowly to the Grange, when a growl from Wolf caused them both to turn; and, looking back into the avenue they had just left, Wilford distinctly saw a crouching figure steal away through the trees.

"A listener!" he exclaimed, angrily, and before Alice could divine or interrupt his purpose, he drew a pistol from his pocket and fired.

He fancied he heared a cry of pain; and Wolf sprang away in the direction taken by the intruder, but returned soon looking greatly disappointed.

"What have you done!" exclaimed Alice, looking as pale as death.

"Taught a spy to keep out of distance for the future," he replied, quietly, "such a scene as ours should be sacred from the prying eyes of vulgar listeners."

Alice trembled at the cool decision of the act; but a few gentle words, and a caress from her lover, reassured her, and they rode on to the Grange.

When they were out of sight, a ruffian, bleeding from a wound in the neck, and with a look of savage fury on his pained and brutal face, emerged from the trees, and limped towards the gate of the grounds.

"Curse you," he muttered fiercely, "that's another grudge to pay you; I've got the cursed ball in my shoulder, and I'll put something round your neck for it. I'll spoil your precious love-making, and you shall soon taste something more bitter than the lips of that lady you seem to like so much."

And shaking his fist with a look of deadly hatred in the direction taken by the boy and Alice, Tiger Blue shrunk away muttering savage curses all the while.

The way to his revenge was clearer now, and soon he meant to seek the aid of one whom he knew would not only be glad to give the gallant youth to justice, but would pay Tiger well for giving him the opportunity.

That one was *Sir Richard Waynecliffe.*

## CHAPTER IX.

### TIGER BLUE LEADS THE OFFICERS TO WAYNCLIFFE GRANGE.

TIGER BLUE was very careful in the means he took to make sure of capturing the Boy Highwayman.

Having seen that he was staying at the Grange, the ruffians had dispatched one of the officers to London for further assistance, well knowing that Wilford would fight to the last.

Then there was Selim and the black mastiff; it would keep a few fully occupied to overcome the resistance they would make in favour of their master. While Hunter went to Bow Street on this errand, Tiger undertook to watch the Grange, in case the boy should depart, and be *non est* by the time Hunter returned with his men.

With this view the traitor had lurked near the Grange, and while doing duty for the first time, on his self imposed task, got a bullet in his shoulder.

He certainly had not included that in his arrangement; but there it was, and, like most uninvited visitors, it would persist in staying a longer time than was agreeable.

The ruffian went to a doctor, who seemed quite to like the idea of poking it about with a long instrument of torture; he called it a probe, and Butler, who went with Tiger, called it a howling machine, which, to judge by the effect it had on the individual operated on, was the most correct term for it.

However, the ball came out at last to Tiger's immense gratification, who didn't care to give it a perpetual residence; and the operation being over, Tiger paid the operator, and dexterously contrived to pick his pocket at the same time.

While Wilford had people outside looking after his interests with so much kind consideration, there were those within the Grange who were quite attentive a quiet way.

Sir Richard Wayncliffe had a tolerable clear and accurate idea as to who and what Wilford was; on more than one occasion he had been compelled to give his purse and jewels to the boy's kind keeping; and the baronet had a remarkable ear for voices.

But he kept his suspicions to himself, thinking that it might not be advisable to awaken any hostile feelings on the boy's part towards himself; so, like a prudent gentleman, he awaited his opportunity.

He could plainly see that Wilford was not deceived by the tale as to the mark upon his brow, although the circumstance was not alluded to again.

But Wilford's presence was dangerous, both to his safety and his interest.

The boy could at any moment touch the train that would blow to the wind every hope of that for which he had stained his soul in crime, and again he stood in the way of his project with regard to Alice.

"They were together always now, and Lord Wayncliffe seemed rather pleased than otherwise at the affection they evidently began to feel for each other.

This puzzled the baronet greatly; his brother, he knew, was a proud man, and one who on all occasions strictly enforced the laws of etiquette, yet he actually gave tacit encouragement to the love growing between his niece and the young stranger, who might, for all he knew, be a mere adventurer.

He ventured once to point this out in very careful terms, of course; for, generous as was the peer to him, he would brook no interference with his doings.

He merely smiled at what he thought was a token of unnecessary anxiety arising out of the baronet's regard for his niece, and said—

"Let them love each other if they like. Why should they not? besides, I am satisfied he is a gentleman—he wears the king's ring!"

"Indeed!" exclaimed Sir Richard, startled by the unexpected intelligence.

"But even that does not answer for his name and birth."

"Pshaw! he has the beauty and bearing of a prince; and, to say the truth, dresses in a style that no prince of the blood ever equalled; then, again, look at his horse, it is worth five thousand at the least!"

"It is a superb animal, unquestionably, but I have heard of a highwayman who rides just such another."

Lord Wayncliffe began to get slightly angry.

"Do not misconstrue my motives," said his brother, plausively, "I like Mr. Leander very much, and feel as you do—that we owe him our deepest gratitude; but for the sake of Alice it would be wise to know more of him before this attachment goes too far."

"How shall we get the information? Is he not my guest? Have we seen anything in his conduct that gives us the right to question him? No! We find that he has all the bearing and accomplishments of a gentleman—he has done us a great service, and I do not believe but that he is everything he should be."

"Nor I, Godfrey; do not think I speak with any motive, save that of care for Alice; still, he may not be what he seems, and we might make the discovery too late."

"Never mind, Richard, I know you speak with the best intention, but it is not wise to anticipate an evil; it is not in my nature to suspect any one, least of all one who is on such terms as our young friend; I would not lose him for the world! I like him; Alice loves—I think so at least—and I will not intrude upon their happiness by expressing ugly doubts, or forcing Mr. Leander to speak of things which he may wish to leave unspoken."

Sir Richard turned away to hide a scowl.

"Listen!" continued his brother, "hear them now; their voices blend together like one chord of rich music—a love song too!—shall we go and look at the singers?"

He took the baronet's arm, and they went towards the drawing-room, passing on their way an apartment in which Lord Horton was striding up and down, puffing savagely at a huge cigar, and howling in between the puffs as though he gave his own melody decided preference.

He was to be pitied still, despite his weaknesses and vices; drunkard and reprobate as he was he could not intrude his presence in the room where sat the maiden with her young companion; and he began to feel some sense of shame when thinking how despicable he must appear when compared by her with the young companion who was now by her side.

So he paced up and down the long lonely room, envying the youth who could by a word or a look gain a smile, which he, with all his wealth and title, had tried in vain to win.

He hated Wilford, but he feared him too; and he hated him more now, while listening to his voice as it blended with the maiden's low sweet tones. His lordship howled "a boy!" to himself, occasionally, and tried to think that he, too, was musical and happy; but the thought was not well expressed by his voice—so after a while he hurled his cigar through the window, stuck both hands in his pockets, and whistled in a manner that showed he felt particularly miserable.

"I believe old Dick only brought me down here to make me look like an ass," he muttered with an oath, "and that cursed dog, too, laid hold of me this morning and nearly took a piece out of my leg! I'll go away. I'll get the girl and go away. Nobody likes me; and the old lord looks at me till I feel as though I'd dined off an iceberg, and drank from icicles. The lady's worse still! She don't even look at me! says "good morning, my lord," and about as many words at night. The other fellow's always with her; whose he, I should like to know? I wish he wasn't quite so strong, I'd smash him!" and here his lordship went to the door and hit the panel with his fist, a proceeding which appeared to relieve his mind, though it took the bark off his knuckles.

Meanwhile, Lord Wayncliffe and his brother had entered the drawing-room.

The song had just ceased, but Alice still stood by the harp, and the strings were yet trembling beneath her slender fingers, while Wilford stood by her side, with his arm tightly placed around her waist.

Their faces were not turned towards the door, so they did not observe the entrance of the peer and his companion, who stood looking on the scene with widely different feelings.

# THE EXTRAORDINARY CONFESSIONS

OF A

## TICKET-OF-LEAVE MAN;

Disclosing the remarkable events of his career—his first crime and punishment—his admission, through his associates, to the dens of London, the gambling-hells, thieves'-kitchens, &c. The curious account of his presentation at Court, and his subsequent adventures and hair-breadth escapes, and, lastly, how he procured his Ticket-of-leave, of which the following is a true copy :—

No. 7,020.

*Order of License to a Convict made under the Statute*
*16 & 17 Vict., chap. 99, sect. 9.*

WHITEHALL,
*13th* day of *May*, 1862.

HER MAJESTY is graciously pleased to grant to *Richard Parker, Norfolk Island*, who was convicted of *Garrotting* at the *Central Criminal Court* on the *5th* day of *April*, 1853, and was then and there sentenced to be Transported beyond the Seas for the term of *Twenty-one* years, Her Royal License to be at large in the United Kingdom, from the day of his liberation under this Order during the remaining portion of his said term of Transportation, unless it shall please Her Majesty sooner to revoke or alter such License. And Her Majesty hereby orders that the said *Richard Parker* be set at liberty within Thirty days from the date of this Order.

Given under my Hand and Seal.

Signed, G. GREY.

J. JEBB,    *Chairman of the Directors*
           *of Convict Prisons.*

---

**OFFICE: 125, FLEET STREET.**

www.ingramcontent.com/pod-product-compliance
Lightning Source LLC
Chambersburg PA
CBHW082052220626

47052CB00006B/1217